Isabella

A Girl of Muslim Spain

Yahiya Emerick

Based on an idea by M. Saeed Dehlvi

Although the book is based loosely upon the character created by M. Sayeed Dehlvi, we have written a completely new version of the story. It is written in a way that is sure to be more appealing to Western literary tastes. Only a small amount of the elements of the original story have been retained and these amount to merely a few names and turns of plot.

Visit www.amirahpublishing.com to learn more

ISBN: 1450541011
EAN-13: 9781450541015

1

In the Secret Garden

"I hope no one sees us, Rosa!"

"Don't worry." Rosa replied. "We haven't been caught yet."

Quickly, the two friends, Rosa and Maria, turned down the street leading to Isabella's house. They passed a few outdoor vendors selling bread, jewelry and cloth, but didn't stop to buy.

When they reached the right home, they entered through the front gate in time to find Isabella coming out to meet them.

"Greetings, Isabella!" they called.

"Greetings, Rosa! Hi, Maria!" she waved back. "My lessons are finished for the day. Let's go!"

Together the three friends left the courtyard and bounded down the street excitedly towards a very special place for them: the *Junaina* garden of Cordoba.

"I hope we get to our secret spot before the gardeners come," remarked Rosa.

"Yes, we'd better hurry," replied Isabella. After several minutes, the trio reached the entrance to the park and continued briskly towards their secret hide-out.

This particular garden was famous for its marvelous beauty: colorful flower beds, low-hanging trees and comfortable benches lined its narrow paths. A veritable chorus of fresh scents, of rose, violet and green leaves, intermingled in a harmony of perfumed fragrance, and several small fountains, placed at regular intervals, provided instant, refreshing water to passers-by.

Wildlife was also abundant. Each dawn, birds awakened residents for half a block, with their light, happy songs. Squirrels and other small mammals made their presence felt as well. Throughout the day they could be seen darting in and out of the shadows, engrossed in their secret missions. Although it wasn't more than a few dozen acres, set near the edge of the city, many were the people who remarked that it was like a piece of Paradise that had fallen to earth.

The three girls walked side by side and talked of their boring tutors and market excursions. Isabella, who strode in the center, was a slender maiden of not more than sixteen or seventeen. She wore a light blue dress that draped around her shoulders once and fell back behind her in a wrap. Her medium length auburn hair lay upon her shoulders like liquid gold frozen in its plummet.

Some called her an angel, for she had a very beautiful face, and many were the well-to-do who asked for her hand. But her father, the Cardinal of Cordoba, always refused. He wanted her to follow the example of the Virgin Mary. Eventually, he would enroll her in a convent, [1] but for now Isabella had only her religious studies to interrupt her days of leisure.

Flanking her on either side walked her two closest friends, Maria and Rosa. Maria always wore dark blue dresses, someone said it was her color, and Rosa was clothed in an off-white wrap-around similar to Isabella's. The clap of their wood and leather soled shoes echoed upon the cobblestones as they walked. The three were very fond of talking and would meet in the garden several times a week.

The girls followed the main path for a few minutes, then turned down a side path. They paused for a moment to gaze at the Amir's castle, just across the river that ran along the eastern border of the park. They took in the beautiful sight and almost lost themselves in thought.

Then they continued on until they reached a cluster of white-blossomed trees. After making sure no one was watching, they stepped behind the trees and entered a thicket of brambles and other tangled bushes. But within this seemingly impenetrable

---

[1] A place young Christian girls are sent to teach them how to be nuns. They are not allowed to leave or get married. They lead lives of prayer and fasting.

barrier there was an open space nearly six feet in diameter. No one else knew about it, not even the gardeners.

The girls discovered it by chance one day when they heard strange sounds coming from behind the bushes. When they had investigated, they found a crawl space through the brambles and an opening inside. In that small sanctuary they happened upon a mother cat and her three kittens. Each girl got one.

The three friends spread a small sheet they brought and were just beginning some serious gossip when they overheard voices.

"*Shhhh. Quiet,*" Maria whispered to the others. "Somebody's near."

"Do you think it's the gardeners?" asked Rosa.

"If they find out we're back here, we'll be in *big trouble,*" remarked Isabella.

Carefully, the girls peered out through the foliage to see who it was. About five yards away sat two men on a gray stone bench. One looked like a *Sheikh,* a Muslim scholar, for he wore a great beard and a simple white robe with a head covering draped loosely over his hair. The other was a younger man, probably a merchant by his fine clothing, and he had a very closely trimmed beard.

"Let's listen to what they're saying," Rosa whispered. The three girls leaned closer and heard the young man speaking first.

"Paul wrote in one of his letters that religious law is a curse and that Jesus, [2] *may he be blessed,* came to relieve people of this *curse.* [3] Now what does *that* mean?" asked the merchant.

The Sheikh laughed, "Umar, you want to get an answer from me when even Christian *priests...*"

Isabella's eyes widened when she heard priests being mentioned.

"These Muslims must be talking about our religion," she whispered excitedly. *"Let's keep listening."*

"Ever since the Muslims came here our religion has been in danger," Maria remarked.

"Shhhh," hushed Isabella. *"Let's listen to what they're saying."*

"Sheikh Samir, you said that Christian priests don't even understand it. Does this mean they're following their religion without understanding it?"

The Sheikh adjusted his head covering and replied, "Just put the question to some important priest and see what they say. But first tell me your biggest problem with what Paul wrote."

Umar adjusted his posture and replied, "Well, there isn't any one problem that I can pinpoint. I just

---

[2] 'Isa (sometimes spelled 'Esa) is the name of Jesus in Islamic terms. Muslims do not believe he was a god or a son of god, but a prophet.

[3] Galatians 3:10

want to understand the concepts involved, and since you've talked to their priests a few times, I was hoping you could explain a little of it for me. What I want to know is this: If religious law is a curse, and Prophet Jesus came to relieve people of this *curse,* does this mean that stealing, lying and adultery are allowed for Christians because they no longer need to follow Divine laws?"

"Wait a minute," interrupted Samir. "How are stealing and lying and such related to religious law being a curse? I don't follow you."

"To get to the point," Umar continued, "the Christian writings include religious laws that forbid theft and murder and all kinds of sins, but if these laws are really a curse, then it would actually be wrong to follow them because they are cursed! If what Paul said was correct, then *liberated* Christians are no longer prevented from doing all those bad things because they're *freed from the laws of God*. But as you can see, Christians are like us; they speak out against sins and still follow the religious laws. So either they have the wrong idea about Prophet Jesus' mission on earth, or they're hypocrites!"

Samir took a long, deep breath and smiled, *"Funny...* You want me to clear up the very problem which Christians can't."

"Have you ever put the issue to any Christians?" Umar inquired. "How did they answer?"

"Well, they would either try to explain it away with some nonsense answer, or they seemed perplexed and would give me some poor excuse about *mysteries* and *faith.*"

The two men sat silently for a moment. In the distance the call could be heard for the sunset prayer. Each man repeated the words of the *Adhan* [4] softly to himself until it was finished. Then they rose up and leisurely walked in the direction of a nearby Masjid.

Isabella paid closer attention to the conversation for she was slightly interested in theological issues and felt the weight of the man's arguments. She stormed her mind for some solution she could give if she was ever questioned by men such as these. But she just couldn't find an answer that was sufficient.

Still absorbed by this issue, she and her friends withdrew from the park. She was determined to consult her father. Isabella left her companions at a crossroads and walked in the twilight towards her home in the northern end of the city.

---

[4] Call to prayer to alert people that they should go to the Mosque or *Masjid.*

2

The Question

Isabella, moving at a much slower pace than usual, reached the outskirts of the Christian sector of the city. There was no danger in traveling in the evening, for the streets were wide and well lit with lamps at regular intervals. The Muslim government had thought it important to beautify and improve the city, as new technologies allowed, and therefore spared no expense to this end.

Isabella paused for a moment to watch a leaf fall in the light of one of those glass encased oil-lamps. Realizing she was absorbed in deep thought, she decided against calling on some other friends for a visit and headed straight for home.

She passed through the arched-stone outer-gates of her father's mansion and strode across the small courtyard. She was met at the door by her maidservant who greeted her humbly. Isabella mumbled something in reply and climbed the stairs that led up to her room. Once inside, she fell into an easy chair, put her feet up on a stool and began thumbing idly through a book she found near her.

The maidservant brought a tray of food to Isabella's room and laid it beside her on a small table. But she was so engaged in her study that she barely acknowledged the gesture. The servant quickly withdrew.

Isabella had been studying Apostle Paul's New Testament writings and paid particular attention to his discussion about religious law being a curse. She read them over and over again but couldn't satisfy herself with a reasonable solution. [5]

After several hours passed in deep research and thought, Isabella grew tired and resolved to ask her father in the morning. Surely, he could explain it because he was the highest priest in the city, *a Cardinal,* and was well-respected for his knowledge.

[5] She was comparing the following verses: Matthew 5:16, Romans 4:2, Galatians 2:16 and James 2:14-26.

So, feeling a little more at ease, Isabella nibbled at the tray of fruits and cheeses and then went to bed.

The following day was a Sunday, and Isabella readied herself for the Mass. [6] Rosa and Maria and a few other friends stopped by to pick her up, and the group walked in the beautiful sunshine towards the main cathedral.

Later in the day, after their religious duties were over, Isabella met with her father in his study. He was happy to see her and asked her what chapters of the Bible she had read the previous evening. He took great pride in Isabella's intelligence and was sure she would make a great Abbess, or leader, one day in some future convent.

Isabella kissed his hand and said, "Father, I read Romans, chapter four, and if you'll permit me, I'd like to ask you about a problem I haven't been able to solve."

The high priest reclined back in his leather-bound chair and smiled, "Of course my child. Ask and I shall resolve your difficulty."

Isabella composed herself and began, "Our Lord gave us Ten Commandments in the Old Testament through Prophet Moses. Now, aren't they religious laws?"

"Yes, those are Divine Commandments which every good man must live by to avoid evil."

---

[6] Mass is the Catholic gathering held on Sundays where some Latin phrases and prayers are recited. Worshippers eat bread and drink wine. The belief is that the bread becomes Jesus' flesh and the wine becomes his blood in your mouth. This is called taking communion.

"But didn't Saint Paul say in one of his letters that religious law was *a curse*?"

"Yes, because religious law *is* a curse."

Isabella paused for a moment and then went on, "So if religious law is a *curse*, and Jesus Christ had to come into the world to die in order to save us from this *curse*. Does this mean that *following* religious law is a sin?"

The Cardinal adjusted his black robe and scratched his head, "Of course, religious law *is* a curse. Instead of worrying about following religious laws, Christians should have faith in Christ. Since he was crucified, and died for our sins, religious law is no longer binding upon us for our salvation."

"So, is stealing *allowed* for us?" she asked meekly.

The high priest began to look agitated and angrily replied, "What's that got to do with religious law! My child, you should think more carefully before you ask such questions. Anyone else would think you're foolish."

Isabella leaned away from her father and struggled to look confident in the presence of such an important man.

"Forgive me," she said. "I wasn't clear enough in my reasoning. What I mean is this: the Commandments, which you agree are religious laws, say that we must not steal or kill or disobey parents and many other things. Now Saint Paul called religious law, of which these are a part, a curse. So, to obey the Ten Commandments is an abomination and *not* to steal or kill or disobey your parents is a sin."

"My child," the Cardinal said condescendingly, "you have not yet understood the position of religious law. If we believe in Christ, we will not be judged according to the law."

"But while believing in Christ, don't we still need the laws just as much for guidance and clarification because anyone can say Christ commanded this or wants that or..."

The Cardinal became very angry at his daughter's seeming insolence and demanded, "Who has put these foolish ideas into your head? What devil has put doubt in you?"

Isabella wanted to run to her room, but she dared not to. After pausing a moment, she revealed the conversation she and her friends overheard in the garden.

When she had finished telling her story, her father had calmed a bit and said, "My child, you know those accursed Muslims are infidels and have never fully respected our religion. Criticism of Christianity is the result of Satanic thinking. My child, you should repent at once and resolve never again to listen to the talk of Muslims. They don't care for the truth and belittle the beliefs of others.

"Do you know what their religion is about? Bloodshed is allowed in their beliefs. Just look, in my great grandfather's time they invaded our beloved Spain and killed hundreds of people and are even now pushing their religion on us. Now, I'm certain the Muslims planted these ideas in your mind. If you would have thought of them yourself, you wouldn't have paid them any serious mind, so how can I possibly address them? Leave me now and think well on your mistakes."

Isabella excused herself quietly from the study and felt the shame of having upset her father. But mixed into that feeling was a new sensation. One she couldn't describe. Her objection remained unsatisfied. An important question went unanswered and made some of her beliefs appear shaky.

She paused a moment in the long hallway leading away from the study. Now it seemed as if she were looking at the walls and features of her house for the very first time. She didn't know what to make of this.

The following day she brought the same issue to the attention of one of her tutors. He also failed to tackle the question to her satisfaction and excused himself, mumbling something about repentance and the Blood of the Cross.

She thought she heard some negative references to the female gender in his ramblings but decided to give him the benefit of the doubt. Until now, Isabella thought her personal difficulty in grappling with this dilemma was due to her own lack of knowledge, but she began to realize that this was a serious problem. Skepticism and doubt began to plague her mind.

3
The Letter

A few days later, Isabella and her two friends, Rosa and Maria, met in their secret place in the garden. The afternoon sun stood high in its zenith and warmed the whole city with its sweeping rays. Maria was just commenting on what a lovely day it was when she noticed through the bushes that the two Muslim men they overheard a few days before were returning. The men approached the same stone bench as before and sat themselves down leisurely.

This day, Umar the merchant, was swathed in a handsome cotton outfit of rich earth-tone colors and embroidery. The Sheikh, Samir, was clothed in white robes as before. The three girls simultaneously hushed themselves and peered forward through the interlaced branches of their hidden abode and listened.

"I've heard an interesting bit of news this day," remarked Umar.

"What is it?" Samir asked.

"Do you remember that point about religious law and Paul's writings we discussed some days ago?"

Samir nodded, "Yes."

"Well, it seems that there is a great commotion among the priests about it. It's said that even the Cardinal has become involved. I've heard more than one report that some highly influential Christians are greatly upset that it appears logically *unanswerable*."

"Maybe it's just a coincidence. I'm not aware of anyone else bringing up this point to the Christians. Who could have heard our discussion?"

"I can't explain it either. All I know is that several meetings have been held among the priests and church officials to find a solution. The news comes from trustworthy Christian associates of mine."

Samir rose to his feet and - half grinning - he proclaimed, "Just one objection puts their priests in an uproar! By Allah, the Most Wise, most of the Christian's beliefs are ridiculous. Like the one where they say because Adam sinned all people, you, me, your mother and everyone else is punishable. I ask you, does that belief have any justification in logic or fairness? And then they say that Jesus, peace be upon him, was a god who had to come to earth and die to forgive the sin of Adam. They still refuse to believe that Allah can forgive sins as He wills. They really go against Allah when they make Him seem so weak and pitiable. If any Christians can come forward to answer these even more serious objections, let them come!"

By this time, Umar was bursting with good-hearted laughter, "If the Christians weren't believing in the absurd, who else would? Everyone can understand logic and reason, but there must be a few who talk nonsense. If a Christian could satisfactorily explain how following the laws of God is a curse, I'd convert in a minute!"

Samir regained his seat, "Maybe we can use this commotion to bring a few of those poor, misguided people to the Truth. It's an excellent da'wah opportunity, I think."

"Yes, that's a good idea," affirmed Umar. "Let's publish a banner in which we can list all the theological oddities of Christianity."

"Yes, that's excellent. Then we can stir up the very roots of Spain herself!"

Isabella and her friends listened silently to the discussion but couldn't keep themselves from cracking their knuckles and clenching their fists nervously. Finally, Isabella lost all patience and whispered to her companions, "We must refute their allegations and do everything we can to convince them of the truth of our religion. May our Lord Jesus Christ bring them to our side!"

Rosa replied excitedly, "If we can convert these Muslims it will be a great victory for Christianity."

Maria broke in, "And the Muslims will never be able to raise their heads in this country again!"

The three girls joined hands and whispered rosaries and short prayers to the Virgin Mary and various saints. After several minutes of doing this, Rosa asked Isabella, "These unbelievers are very hot-headed. So how can they be influenced to give up Satan and take the hand of the Lord Jesus? You know that even our priests are afraid to talk religion with them."

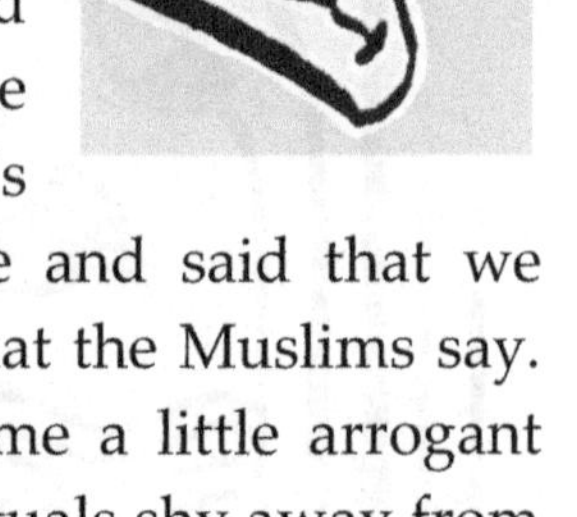

"Yesterday," announced Maria, "I asked my tutor about the religious law and Saint Paul's writings, and he just ignored me and said that we shouldn't pay any attention to what the Muslims say. Why wouldn't the Muslims become a little arrogant when even our priests and intellectuals shy away from them?"

Isabella thought for a moment and replied, "Maybe our priests just don't want to talk to those unbelievers. But in no way does their silence mean that they cannot solve these problems. If they were sure that the Muslims would convert to Christianity after being thoroughly rebutted, I'm sure they would be eager to face them."

Maria nodded, "Yes, written promises from the Muslims should be made and then they could meet with our priests. This way, the priests will be pressured to talk with them and the Muslims will be compelled to embrace our religion when their objections are refuted."

"This is a good plan," said Isabella, "but do you think these Muslims will agree to it?"

"Why not?" answered Rosa. "Look at what we just heard them saying."

"Then let's not wait. Let's tell them right now that they should prepare to meet our priests. I'll write a note which one of you can take to them." With that, Isabella produced a slip of paper, a sealed ink vial, and a long slender writing quill from her purse.

Maria leaned forward as Isabella prepared to write and said, "Do you think we should *ask* the priests first? What if they decline?"

"If the Muslims agree to convert to Christianity when their objections are satisfied," Isabella answered, "then our priests could never refuse to see them." She then wrote the following words.

Respected Muslims,

Please excuse me. I have overheard your discussion on account of the proximity of our places of rest. As I am also a student of theological issues, I pray you will not mind the intrusion. You have just told your companion that if the issue of religious law being a curse were explained satisfactorily to you, you would convert to Christianity. As humble servants of Jesus Christ we gladly accept your challenge, provided you declare your compliance in writing.

- A Humble Christian

Maria took the letter and emerged from the bushes, making sure to keep out of sight of the Muslims. She carefully stepped over the flowers until she regained the nearby path. Walking around the corner of the thicket, she strode confidently towards the two men. Without saying a word, she handed the note to a surprised Umar.

After reading it, he looked up at her, then he handed it to Samir. While Samir was reading, Umar reached inside a pocket for some writing materials. Samir finished reading the letter and set it aside.

"So, is this letter from you my dear young lady?" he asked.

"I am but the messenger," she replied in an even voice. When Umar completed his reply, he handed it carefully to Maria who took it and quickly withdrew.

When she returned to her companions, the trio couldn't open the folded note fast enough. It read:

Dear Anonymous Person,

We thank you for the challenge and agree that if your elders make clear to us the problem of the law of God being a curse, then I assure you that I myself will be the first to embrace your religion. Tell us where and when we shall come for the discussion.

-A Humble Servant of Islam,

Umar AbdulHakim

Isabella wrote one more note that simply said:

I shall inform you tomorrow at this hour as to the time and location.

- A Humble Christian

After Maria delivered it and returned, the three left the garden full of excitement. It was decided that Isabella should make the contacts and arrangements since her father was a Cardinal. And with that settled, the friends bid each other farewell and went down different streets towards their separate homes.

Isabella, however, decided to make a call upon one of her favorite old tutors along the way, Friar Michael. He himself was an ordained priest and Isabella was very fond of his cheerful temperament and happy outlook on life.

He once laughed so loud in a meeting that the former Cardinal censured him and made him retire to the life of a humble monk. Isabella's father, the current Cardinal, dismissed him as a tutor for his daughter after he felt that he wasn't being strict enough with her.

The housekeeper admitted Isabella and quickly showed her to the friar. He was a large man, but not menacingly so. He had an uneven short beard lining his kindly face and wore the brown airy, robe of a humble man of the order. "How may I serve you, my child?" He pleasantly asked.

Isabella dropped into a nearby easy chair and told him about what happened and the plan she devised. The friar, now seated, listened intently, and when she finished, he grinned broadly and laughed, "Ah, my Isabella. You are a wilder storm than any man or priest can tangle with. I'm not well versed enough in knowledge of the mysteries to answer the problem, but I can say that your plan is full of boldness and vigor."

Isabella smiled appreciatively. At least one adult had confidence in her.

After a little more discussion, the Friar agreed to bring the matter to some eminent theologians who were meeting the next day at noon. He also assured her that he could probably arrange a meeting with the Muslims at the same time two days after that. Then, he walked her to the door. But before she left, she grabbed him in a big hug which he returned affectionately and then she scampered through the streets in the direction of her home.

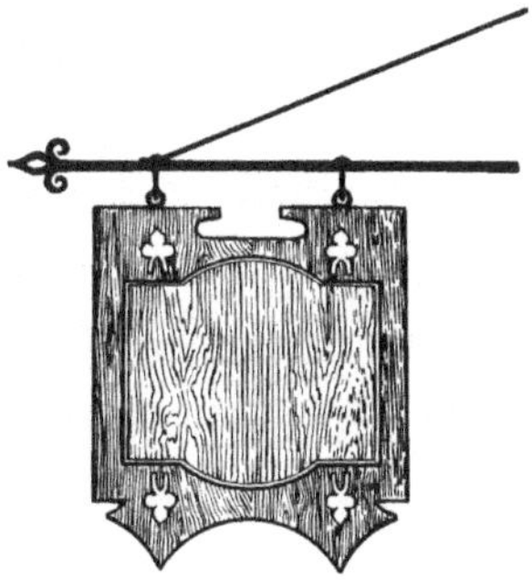

Isabella could barely sleep that night. She was continually haunted by all the things that could go wrong. What if the Christians couldn't produce an effective answer to the objection of the Muslims? Christians would appear foolish and irrational. She tried to put it out of her head.

Then, after a few hours of deep sleep, the first dim rays of dawn appeared. Isabella jumped out of her bed full of energy and purpose. After a hasty breakfast, she excused herself from her father's table and bustled off to her room and began to study the Bible in earnest.

As it was nearing the noon hour, Isabella put aside her work and hurried to Maria's house where the three friends agreed to meet. Maria's father was a famous Christian scholar and theologian and was quite wealthy besides. His large and spacious home was often the scene of many a meeting and today dozens of priests and several theologians were gathering there, as Friar Michael had said.

Maria and Rosa, who were on an upstairs balcony, saw Isabella entering the large door to the main hall and called down to her. The room was full of Christian dignitaries and priests so Isabella had to weave her way carefully to the stairway leading to the second floor. She just made it to her friends in time when down below a hand-bell was rung which signaled the crowd to be seated. Eagerly, the three girls peered over the balcony at the meeting below.

The men sat in chairs that had been arranged in rows while the most important guests sat at a great table opposite them on a raised platform. At the middle of the table was a podium. Behind it stood Maria's father who began to bring the meeting to order.

"My beloved brethren," Father Peter began, "we are gathered in the presence of our Holy Redeemer, Jesus Christ, to seek his wisdom and saving grace. As you all are well aware, a great controversy has been unleashed by Satan. Using every means at his disposal he has caused the Muslims to put doubt into our theology and teachings."

A general murmur of agreement emanated from the crowd. "Our respected brother, Friar

Michael, has informed me that a dialogue has been proposed between the Muslims and our selves by a humble Christian Servant, whom he has declined to name, saying it be the will of Christ."

One of the men seated near Father Peter spoke out, "We were wondering about what we were summoned here for so urgently. Now it is clear that the pressing issue is really quite simple. If we are going to meet and convert the Muslims, call them here and now, and any one of us will convince them."

Another priest replied, "Yes, indeed this is not a grave decision for we often hold discussions with the Muslims. But ever since the news has gone out that Christians have no answer to certain *objections* of the Muslims, the issue before us has assumed great importance. We must prepare ourselves and determine a day at once."

Friar Michael stood up from his seat in the crowd, "Your Eminences!" he said, addressing the high-ranking priests at the table. "Tomorrow is Sunday and many Christians will be gathering at the Great Cathedral. We should call the Muslims to come there that they may be impressed by the multitudes of sincere Christians. And may the Lord Jesus Christ increase the wisdom he bestows upon you surrounded by the glory of his servants."

There was a general nod of agreement from the men and this was confirmed by one of the high priests when he said, "That is an excellent idea. The Cardinal will be present at the Great Cathedral that day and there is no one more learned in all of Spain than he. We may need his wisdom at some stage in our dialogue."

After some more discussion about strategies for answering the *law-curse* issue, the meeting was adjourned, and the priests prepared for the sumptuous meal soon to be served. Isabella, Maria and Rosa left the great hall and met Friar Michael on the way out.

"Aren't you going to stay for the dinner, Friar Michael?" Maria asked.

"No, my child. Our Lord Jesus fasted often and ate but little. I seek to follow in his footsteps; that is all."

Before he left them, he handed Isabella a written permit which would allow Umar and his party to enter the church. The trio took the permit and headed straight to the garden. [7]

When the girls arrived at the meeting place of the two Muslims, they found Umar and Sheikh Samir there, along with several others. Two looked like merchants, one an artist, and the last two were dark-skinned Muslims from across the Straits of Gibraltar.

[7] The Islamic government was responsible for the safety and security of Christian places of worship. Therefore, permission to enter a church had to be obtained from the local priests.

Umar greeted the three young ladies, being quite surprised that they appeared to be the ones who have been arranging things. "Welcome and Peace," he said.

Isabella said nothing in return, out of nervousness or mistrust, she couldn't tell, and handed the permit to Umar who stood up to accept it. He read it aloud to the group then tucked it in his pocket.

Sheikh Samir addressed the girls, "We are thankful for your painstaking efforts and if anyone receives guidance from Allah after this affair, the credit will first go to you."

"These are young scholars of Christian philosophy, and they appear to be well versed in theology. Their zeal is worthy of praise," Umar intoned.

Isabella curtly replied, "We are humble servants of Jesus Christ and thank you for accepting the invitation."

One of the dark-skinned men cried out, "Allah forbid! Just see how the Christians make others equal with Allah and deify Jesus. They're out of their senses because..."

Umar turned to him and interrupted, "My brother, you've brought up another controversy when there is already one to be discussed tomorrow." He then turned to address Isabella, whom he suspected was the leader amongst them, "You may convey to the priests that, Insha'llah, [8] we will be at the church at the appointed hour."

Isabella led her companions away and bid them farewell for the evening, as she had much study and prayer to pursue. While she walked home alone, one thing began to trouble her. "The Muslims will sit with each other no matter what their color or social status," she mused, "while priests would never sit with soldiers or artisans, and certainly not with the poor, darker-skinned Christians from the south." A funny feeling crept into her stomach and she tried not to think of it anymore.

[8] Insha'llah means, "If Allah wills it."

4

The First Meeting

Umar and Sheikh Samir spent much of the evening together at Umar's home studying the Qur'an and the Bible. They took note of important points and discovered several new issues they could bring before the Christians.

Above all, however, they prayed for strength and for the ability to *reason with them in a superior manner,* as the Qur'an commands. After making some final preparations, Umar invited his friend to sleep in the guest room since it was so late in the evening.

Two days later, all of Cordoba was in a buzz. News of the impending summit between Christian and Muslim theologians created an undercurrent of excitement. Everyone had heard of the mysterious Christian who called the meeting and some speculated that it was one of the saints or the Virgin Mary's doing.

Many Christians felt motivated by the event to open debates with their Muslim neighbors about religious issues. But because the average Christian was forbidden by the church to read the Bible, most of these encounters were short-lived.

Muslims, too, began to catch the excitement. For the entire day before the great meeting, people visited the home of Umar and offered him words of support. Finally, the Muslims could declare once and for all the superiority of Islam! On Sunday morning multitudes, both Muslim and Christian, lined the streets and markets and milled about in anticipation.

The priests had not expected such a large throng of people at the Great Cathedral. They were even more surprised to find so many Muslims wanting to come and watch the proceedings. Being fearful of allowing such a mixed gathering into their sacred place, the decision was made to allow a maximum of forty Muslims in the church.

They would be seated in a section near the rear. The rest of the space was reserved for the hundreds of Christian leaders and wealthy people who had come to see their religion vindicated.

As noon approached, people began to take their seats in the huge, cavernous hall. A bell rang out from the tower adjoining the church and the priests began to file into the front from a side room.

The eleven men, all clad in black robes, sat in a half circle facing the audience. On the walls behind the priests were paintings of religious scenes: of Jesus hanging on a cross and bleeding, and of beautiful angels alongside portraits of the Virgin Mary.

The Cardinal entered last and took a seat in the center of the assembled church leaders.

Umar and Sheikh Samir were sitting in the front row whispering to each other.

The elderly Muslim scholar wore a white thobe [9] with a kufi. [10] A green turban was wrapped gently around his head and the ends trailed down behind his back. Umar was dressed in a handsome robe which draped over a loose-fitting pair of pants and a blue over-shirt. A stunning blue turban rested upon his brow which seemed to cause light to reflect from his youthful, friendly face.

Isabella, Maria and Rosa waited tensely for the proceedings to begin. They arrived early and found a seat near the front so they could see everything. Isabella looked towards Umar, but she could only see the side of his face. He didn't appear nervous. Then she looked at her father, the Cardinal, seated in the place of honor. He didn't appear unsettled either.

---

[9] A long shirt-like robe.
[10] A hat.

"What do you think will happen?" Rosa whispered. But a quick glance from Isabella and Maria signaled her to keep quiet.

One of the seated priests stood up from his seat and began chanting something in Latin. Isabella recognized it as a sort of opening benediction to the Blessed Virgin. After he had finished, the crowd of Christians made the sign of the trinity with hand motions and sat silently. The Muslims in the crowd simply stared at the bizarre paintings. Most of them had never *seen* the inside of a church before. A few of them looked at the statues and muttered, "*Astaghfirullah.*" [11]

As if on cue, Friar Michael, Isabella's old tutor, walked out from another room and approached the priests. He bowed towards them and then approached the Cardinal and kissed the ring on his hand. He then retreated a step, keeping his back bent, and then rose and turned to face the crowd-- and the two Muslim guests.

"We are gathered here for an unusual occasion," he bellowed out. "Today, our holy fathers have decided to put an end to all doubts and misunderstandings about the most holy and Catholic Christian religion. Today we are going to arrive at the truth and then we will all bow down upon our knees to the one power in the universe, the Lord Jesus Christ."

---

[11] *"Allah forgive. (such evil things that people do)."*

Many of the Christians murmured little prayers and looked on the Friar with approval and respect. The Muslims in the audience remained stone-faced.

"I call upon the one who names himself Umar AbdulHakim to come forward."

"And also upon Sheikh Samir Al Adhami." Added Umar quickly.

"We shall speak this day only to Umar," Friar Michael responded haughtily.

Umar looked nervously at Samir who glanced back at Umar and nodded confidently, "You're a sharper edge than I am, Umar."

Umar turned to the priests and whispered to himself, *"Allah help me in this endeavor."* He then walked to the front of the church and took a chair at a small table facing the priests.

Friar Michael, who stood in the space between Umar and the church leaders, walked forward and said, "Umar, we have learned that you have some doubts about the truth of Christianity. We have also learned that you have sworn to convert to this religion if those doubts could be resolved. Is this true?"

Umar leaned forward in his seat and answered, "By Allah, it is true that I doubt your religion and if those doubts could be satisfied to the point that they could not be denied, then I would have no choice but to the follow the truth."

Friar Michael then nodded his head at Umar and retreated to a chair a few feet to his left. One of the assembled priests then stood up and approached

Umar slowly. He clasped his hands together behind his back and paced a few steps in front of him. Maria recognized the man as her father, Peter, and nudged Isabella excitedly.

"I am told that your most serious doubt is Paul's labeling of religious law as a curse. *Is that true*?" Peter asked rather condescendingly.

Umar nodded in the affirmative and Peter continued, "But this is such a minor issue. You *Mozzlems,* as I understand it, believe in your Qur'an, so what I propose is simple: that the basis of Christianity and Jesus Christ should be decided by the Qur'an *itself.* Do you *approve*?"

Umar turned his head to Samir who shrugged his shoulders in bewilderment. A Christian who sat near to Isabella whispered to a friend, "This man, father Peter, is an expert on the *Mozzlem* religion and knows Arabic. He's going to lay a trap for that infidel from his own book." Isabella sat straighter and watched intently.

Umar looked Peter in the face and replied, "Even though our discussion was supposed to be on the subject of religious law, I can see you would rather not discuss it. And since I know of no other book that I would rather discuss than Allah's last revelation to humanity, then we can move to the subject of Jesus in the Qur'an if you like."

Peter looked slightly annoyed and stated, "Don't worry; we will answer your question about religious law. But first, for the benefit of the people who have come here seeking knowledge." Peter raised his arms and extended them over the crowd, "I would like to start with the most basic issues which divide our communities."

"So be it," responded Umar confidently.

"Very well. To begin with, doesn't your Qur'an call Jesus Christ the spirit or *ruh* of God and ***The Word*** or *kalam* of God? And doesn't your Qur'an say that Jesus gave life to the dead and was raised up to heaven? Then if you believe in the Qur'an, how can you doubt that the Lord Jesus is the Son of God?"

The Christians let out a cheer of approval for Peter's opening attack and hugged one another in joy. The priests looked on their fellow scholar with confidence and the Muslims sat up straighter in their seats. Samir looked at Umar who appeared calm.

Umar rose to his feet, causing the crowd to quiet themselves. He looked Peter in the eyes and responded in a bold and strong voice, "Actually, the Qur'an uses the term *Ruh* to apply to many different things, and not one of them has anything to do with *being* Allah. And the Qur'an calls Jesus ***a word*** from Allah and not ***The Word,*** in the sense that He can create Jesus, or a hundred Jesus' with a mere word. *'Kun fayya kun.' 'Be and it is.'* And the Qur'an states that Jesus revived the dead *with Allah's permission* and that Allah raised Jesus to Heaven to protect him from being killed by the Jews. Jesus was never crucified or killed and Allah certainly does not give birth to children." [12]

The Muslims erupted in cheers this time and slapped each other on the back heartily. The Christians merely shifted themselves back and forth and grumbled. Peter recovered from his momentary setback and tried a new approach.

"You claim that Jesus was never crucified, that he did not die on the cross. If he did not die, then how do you expect God to forgive us our sins? It is the saving blood of Jesus which atones for the dark stain we inherited from Adam. Jesus had to die *as a god* to make up for the ultimate crime of humanity. How does your Qur'an answer that?" sneered Peter smugly.

"You're bringing us to the most fundamental differences of faith and are shifting the discussion even further by taking the cover of the Qur'an. If you insist on our beliefs being the issue here, then we will have to decide whether or not Adam committed an unpardonable sin, and if it is decided that he did, we will have to discuss whether it could, indeed, be passed on to every generation of people and doom everyone to being naturally evil.

"Then we will have to debate how this infectious sin can be removed. Then you will have to prove that Jesus was Allah and that only by Allah coming here, or at least one-third of him, and literally

---

[12] See Qur'an 5:72-75.

committing suicide by allowing His creatures to kill him, can people be saved. And then beyond that you will have to prove that Jesus, in fact, died and spent three days in Hell. All these things that your religion teaches cannot be proved from the Qur'an, even as your own Bible is not clear about them, so I suggest we go back to our original topic."

Peter looked visibly shaken by Umar's strong reply and the Christians in the audience fidgeted uneasily. Isabella forgot that she wasn't breathing and gulped some air. For a fraction of an instant she agreed with what Umar had said, but then she caught herself mentally.

"All this is irrelevant," Peter waved his arm dismissively, "I simply wish to prove from the Qur'an that Jesus is the word and spirit of God and that, therefore, Christianity has a solid foundation."

Umar responded, "Considering that that's impossible, as I just showed you, I can see that we're in danger of going nowhere with our conversation."

Peter turned to face the Cardinal, who bent his head slightly in some secret exchange of instructions. Peter smiled wryly and called out loud, "Very well. I shall call upon the one, the mysterious Christian servant who brought us all together, to stand and refresh our memories about the subject of today's proceedings."

Isabella felt her heart drop from its resting place. Her identity was going to be revealed! How could her father have allowed this? Peter, meanwhile, pointed his finger at Isabella, who meekly rose from her seat. All eyes turned upon the fragile young girl. Isabella felt their weight crushing her.

"Tell this, this *Umar,* what we are discussing here today?" Peter commanded.

Isabella looked at her friends for support then softly said, "We are here to talk about whether Christians need to follow the divine laws and religious commandments of their religion."

Her voice quivered and her throat felt dry. She swallowed hard then continued. "The argument is that if religious law is a curse, are Christians wrong in wishing to follow it. But I believe that Father Peter's first issue for you is also worthy of discussion. I think that after he has dealt with your objection then you should deal with his."

Umar looked at the nervous young girl kindly and replied, "I shall leave the ground open for you. I promise that when my objections are dealt with, we will answer any general questions you may have. But if, as I have promised, I will convert to Christianity, then who will need to ask more questions?" And for an instant, their eyes focused on each other. Isabella felt strangely calmed and quickly turned her head away.

"Well then," Peter said, calling Umar's attention back. "What problem do you see with religious law being a curse?"

"If you'll respond to each one of my questions, I feel the matter will be solved in no time."

Peter nodded in the affirmative. Isabella, in the mean time, had regained her seat and felt sick in her stomach. She was angry that her father would betray her like that. Maria put her arm around her friend and Rosa took Isabella's hand and squeezed it with concern.

"To begin," Umar said, "Are the laws you teach which forbid your people to steal, lie and fornicate, etc... considered matters relating to religious law?"

"Of course, they are," intoned the priest.

"And just what is Saint Paul's opinion about religious law?"

"That depends on what you mean by opinion."

"I think you know what meaning I intend, but since you have chosen to be evasive, I will specify. Saint Paul labeled religious law a curse in the book of Galatians. Is this true?"

"Yes, but you're missing the main point. He was saying that following religious law for the sake of salvation was wrong, for only the blood of Christ Jesus can bring salvation. When Christ died, he saved us from having to follow the law by atoning for our wickedness. A Christian does not need to concern himself with following a detailed code of conduct, like you *Mozzlems*, but only needs to follow a few general rules based on love and faith in Jesus."

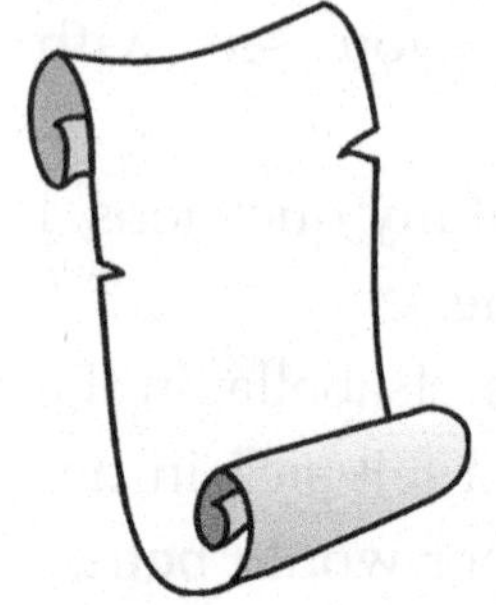

A new feeling of confidence passed over the Christian spectators and Father Peter felt a flush of pride at his seemingly well orchestrated answer. Umar, however, was not to be denied his goal and he reiterated, "But why the need to follow *a few rules* at all, and who decides which rules they will be? For I have seen one group of Christians say *do this and this* and you will be saved and I have seen other Christians saying to do the opposite things to be saved.

"And further," Umar went on, "what about the discarded laws? What about Allah's laws and society? Have they no place in our lives or do you really believe that Allah can have no place in detailing how people govern their social and personal lives in communities? Doesn't your book tell you to follow whoever is in charge of you, whether they are of your religion or not? What good is your beliefs if you don't even have a way to form a true social order? No wonder Christian laws are a joke! They don't exist for you."

The weight was back again with Umar and Father Peter realized it. In an effort to buy time to formulate an adequate response the priest stalled with a question of his own, "Where did you get the notion that we believe people do not need to follow God's commands?"

"Well," Umar began, "your own Bible says that,

> *'Everyone must submit himself to the governing authorities, for there is no authority except that which God has established. The authorities that exist have been established by God. Consequently, he who rebels against the authority is rebelling against what God has instituted...'* [13]

"So, does this mean that the governing authorities, whoever they may be, can tell you Christians how to live your public and social lives? If you really believe this verse then you have to follow the laws of Islam, because we Muslims now control this land! Who among you decides how to follow your religion if you care for no laws and talk about mysteries and faith all the time? I have seen with my own eyes, priests telling rules to people and warning them that hell will come for those who don't follow them! Where is your faith then?"

When Umar finished his words, the hall was silent. Christians looked on in disbelief and Muslims were spellbound by the logic of what they just heard. Peter was also speechless momentarily. He shakily replied, "You cannot understand these mysteries without the help of the Holy Ghost, and just because

---

[13] Romans 13:1-2

you don't understand something doesn't mean it's wrong. Saint Paul was calling earthly laws a curse and not all laws in general, and certainly not Divine laws."

"All right, I'll accept that line of reasoning for a moment." Umar intoned. "Now tell me, are the laws against stealing, cheating and killing *earthly laws* or *Divine laws*?"

"You're not understanding my point. Just listen. What our Lord Jesus Christ said is more important than what Paul, who was a man like us, wrote. Our Lord ordered us to follow the commandments as contained in the Old Testament. [14] But he *died* to save us from being *judged* by that standard."

"Wait a minute," Umar objected, "Now you're telling me that one part of the Bible is better than the other?"

"What do you mean?"

"If you're telling me the sayings of Jesus are better than the sayings of Paul, but they are both in the same Bible that you say is the Word of God, then I think you need to take a serious look at how your Bible was made and put together. I even read that your Bible wasn't made until 300 years after Jesus! And furthermore, if Jesus commanded you to follow the laws, then who is this *Saint Paul* to call them a curse? How can anyone say that God's own laws are

---

[14] Matthew 5:19 and 10:25.

not a good standard for Him to judge us? Look at Matthew 19:17 in your own book and read it! [15] I dare you right now!"

Father Peter angrily grabbed a Bible off the front table and read the words Jesus was supposed to have said, "*...but if you will enter into life, keep the commandments.*" [16]

When he had finished reading, Umar looked up at the ceiling and announced, "I'm afraid my objections grow stronger while you grow more confused."

Cheers erupted from the Muslims and shouts of "*Allahu Akbar*" [17] could be heard. The Christians began to fidget in their seats and a few people got up and left the cathedral. Isabella felt as if she were frozen in a trance and Maria and Rosa sat by in silence.

"You need the Holy Ghost," mumbled Father Peter.

"How can a *ghost* solve the problem of Jesus saying to follow the laws and Paul saying they're a curse. Why have all these teachings about Jesus *dying to save people* when it seems that Jesus only wanted people to have sincere faith and to follow the commandments of God!

---

[15] Matthew 19:16-17 states that a man asked Jesus, "...Good Master, what good things shall I do, that I may have eternal life? And he (Jesus) said unto him, Why callest thou me good? There is none good but One, that is God: but if thou will enter into life, keep the commandments." Clearly, Jesus was saying he wasn't God and that the laws must be obeyed for salvation.

[16] Also see Romans 13:9.

[17] "Allah is Great!"

"All we know is that our Lord directed us to respect the laws of the Old Testament. But salvation cannot be gained by merely following the laws without the Atonement for the sin of Adam."

"So, Prophets Moses, David, Noah and others must have missed their chance for salvation, because all they had was faith in God and following the religious laws Allah gave them. They had no Jesus dying to atone for the sins of Adam."

"Before Christ came, all they had was the religious law for their salvation, but the atonement of Jesus changed all that for us. We don't need to have the good works that come from following the law."

Umar stood up and looked Peter in the eyes, "But Paul wrote, "***Faith without works is dead***." If we don't follow the religious laws of God then crying about faith in Jesus is worthless. It's not atonement that brings salvation, but faith in God and doing what's right— as explained in religious law!"

The Muslims jumped to their feet shouting, *"Allahu Akbar! Allahu Akbar!"* Isabella felt a hot flash rush through her body and her forehead and palms became sweaty. Maria slumped back and Rosa cupped her face in her hands. Clearly, the Christian side suffered a setback.

"Order," shouted Peter. "Come to order!"

A few moments passed before the people settled themselves down again. "It is blasphemy to shout in the house of the Lord! It is clear that you," Peter pointed to Umar, "are unable to understand these mysteries. Our means of salvation are the Divinity of Christ and his death and atonement for our sins. Our Lord Christ suffered for our guilt and by his grace gave us salvation."

Umar raised his right arm and said, "You have failed to answer my objection. Therefore, I remain unsatisfied. I cannot accept your beliefs nor can I say that you explained them to my satisfaction."

Isabella stood to her feet so quickly it surprised even her. She pushed forward and called out in a loud voice, "I came here to listen to this discussion and I know I have no say in any matter. But I beg of your Eminences, please, do not let the issue *die here*."

The priests looked on the young girl gravely and a silence fell over the chamber at her words. The Cardinal whispered to the priests next to him and finally Friar Michael was called to the front for instructions.

Umar looked back at Sheikh Samir who nodded encouragingly; then he turned his head in the other direction at Isabella and considered her strength of character. Isabella caught his glance and looked away quickly. But something caused her to raise her eyes once more and she looked at Umar, in his eyes, calmly. Just then, Friar Michael returned from his consultations with the Cardinal and motioned for the people to pay attention.

"My Brothers!" he began. "We have assembled ourselves here to search for truth, and it is certainly a difficult task. But for it to succeed there must be a sincere heart and an urge to accept the truth. The question of faith shows that no one can succeed by his own effort. We should, therefore, pray to God that He should reveal to us, with the help of the Holy Ghost, the mysteries of the Christian faith."

Some Christians in the audience felt reassured and whispered a few quiet *amens*. Others just sat there.

"Brothers!" Friar Michael continued. "The question of whether or not religious law is a curse is irrelevant. The real difficulty is that our Muslim overlords know nothing about our Christian religion and, therefore, they try to engage us in philosophy. The essence of our faith can be described in two terms: Divinity of Christ and Atonement. Whoever understands this knows the mysteries of our faith. So, I hereby request that our Muslim friends here give up talking about philosophy and agree to engage us on the truth of the Divinity of our Lord Jesus Christ."

"Considering that you could not answer our questions thus far," Umar responded. "What makes you think you will do any better on another issue?"

"We have not failed here," Friar Michael intoned, "You have simply not understood. We are confident on a simpler issue you will see the truth of our religion and embrace the most holy and Catholic faith."

"I accept your challenge, as any seeker after truth should."

"It is now mid day and I think it would be wise to end the proceedings for now," Father Peter announced.

"Then we can continue after we have all had our lunch and rest," added Sheikh Samir, firmly.

"But you have to offer your noon prayers, *don't you*?" Father Peter blurted out, in a way that did not at all sound like he was worried over the religious obligations of his foes.

"We can offer them here, in your church."

Father Peter and the rest of the priests were taken aback. "*Muslims,* offering prayers in our church!" one priest cried. The Cardinal whispered to Father Peter who in turn addressed the gathering, "It has been decided. We will close the meeting for today and will continue it next Sunday at the same time."

The crowd gasped in surprise and some people began to grumble.

"Why should we wait a week to continue?" Umar called out.

Father Peter spread both arms in front of himself and replied condescendingly, "Don't we all have other things which also require our attention?"

"I think no other business can be as important as this."

Seeing that both the Christians and Muslims in the audience were agitated by the thought of a long delay in solving this controversy, the Cardinal stood up and announced, "Very well, we shall continue this meeting tomorrow at the residence of Father Peter. I am afraid that because of the smaller space only church leaders may attend and no more than four Muslims."

The crowd was clearly angry realizing that few of them would be able to attend the next day's session. The ushers and other church workers did their best to control the situation but were having a hard time holding the people back. The Cardinal raised his hand and shouted for the guards to move the people out of the cathedral. Slowly, the people jostled their way out of the main doors and spilled out onto the street, shouting and babbling.

Umar and Sheikh Samir were surrounded by the happy and jubilant Muslims and were whisked off to the Masjid for the noon prayer. Shouts of *"Allahu Akbar"* could be heard fading away down the street.

Isabella watched Umar being lifted on the shoulders of his companions and stared blankly at her own Christian brethren milling about in front of the cathedral arguing with each other and shouting. Christianity was damaged today and she knew it. With her two friends by her side, she walked home in silence.

5

The Showdown

Monday came, and Isabella arose from her fitful sleep. She still couldn't make sense out of what she saw the previous day. She had wanted to prove to Muslims that Christianity was the truth, but instead, her own beliefs were shaken. She felt an emptiness inside like she had never felt before. And the way that Muslim merchant, Umar, so easily answered the most learned men she had ever known. Then she remembered how his eyes met hers, and she shook her head to clear her mind.

Although today's meeting was restricted to Church leaders and well-to-do Christians, Isabella could attend because it was being held at her friend's house. Rosa would probably be there too. Isabella got out of bed and washed her face in silence. A moment later a knock at the door signaled to her that her breakfast had come. The maidservant entered the room carrying a tray with fruit, bread and cheese on it and left it on the dresser. Quietly, she retreated out the door and closed it behind her.

Thankful for the distraction, Isabella began to nibble on the food. It tasted bland. She dressed herself in an off-white skirt and blouse and picked out an appropriate vest from her closet.

When she was ready, she picked up her hand bag and left her home for Maria's house. She knew her father, the Cardinal, would already be there preparing with other scholars.

Along the way, Isabella bought some apples from a street vendor and a new vial of ink from a small store. The people she met seemed distracted and absent-minded. "Everyone must be miffed about not being able to attend the *showdown* today," she thought.

When she arrived, Maria and Rosa greeted her at the door and ushered her past the roving priests to the upstairs balcony from where they could watch. "What do you think will happen today?" Rosa asked.

"Indeed, I do hope our side does better this time," Maria added.

Isabella paused in her thoughts and then replied, "I honestly don't know. Umar is pretty clever and eloquent besides." She felt a rush of adrenaline when she mentioned the Muslim merchant and realized that it was the first time she ever said his name.

"I wonder where he learned all the things he did?" Rosa asked.

The doorman announced, "The *Mozzlems* have arrived!"

A puff of excitement seemed to enter the room as the priests and wealthy Christians scrambled to find their seats. There were at least thirty men present and about five women. The women were seated along one wall and the men filled the rest of the large room. At the long table in the front stood Father Peter, the Cardinal and two other men. Father Peter called out to the doorman, "Bring them in."

From their balcony at the top of the stairs, the three girls watched as four Muslims entered the chamber. Umar and Sheikh Samir were followed by two people, a tall man and a woman wearing a tan-colored scarf, or *hijab*.

They both seemed to be merchants, like Umar. When the group passed into the aisle, the doorman stopped and said, "Only Umar is permitted to go further. The rest of you will sit in these three seats in the back." He motioned to three crude and uncomfortable chairs in the very back.

"By Allah! These people have no hospitality!" grumbled the Muslim sister.

"We *are* their guests and must accept the best they can offer." The Sheikh responded. "We will sit there."

The Sheikh and the two merchants sat down and the doorman escorted Umar towards the front where a lone, small chair stood facing the main table.

Umar sat down and waited. His back was towards the balcony, so Isabella couldn't get a good look at his face. She felt a little annoyed. They should have at least given him a better chair!

Father Michael entered the room and briefly conferred with the Cardinal at the head table. Then, he turned around and took a chair near the back. Isabella could see he was irritated. What happened? She would find out later.

Father Peter arose and everyone quieted down. "My brothers in Christ, we are here under the watchful eyes of the Virgin Mary and the saints to prove to the *Mozzlems* the truth of the divinity of Christ. In so doing, we will convert them to our religion and will welcome them as new members in the body of the church.

"As we agreed, we will be discussing the divinity of our Lord Jesus Christ and the need for Atonement today. Would you like to say anything before we proceed?"

Umar stood up and replied, "Yes." He paused for a moment and began to recite, in Arabic, verses from Surah Al Furqan. [18] When he finished, he translated them thus:

[18] Qur'an 25: 1-3.

"In the Name of Allah,
the Compassionate Source of All Mercy.

"Blessed is the One Who sent down the Standard (of right and wrong) to His servant to be a warning to the universe. To Him belongs the dominion of space and the earth. He has not given birth to a son nor does He have a partner in dominion. He created all things and ordered them perfectly.

"Yet, they have taken besides Him gods that can create nothing but are themselves created; that have no control to protect or bring good to themselves. Nor can they control death, life or resurrection."

When she heard these beautiful words being recited, Isabella felt weak and leaned against her friends. They helped her sit down on the balcony floor and Rosa held her hand tightly. "That was beautiful," Maria whispered.

"Why don't they ever translate the Latin our priests recite in church at Mass?" Rosa commented.

Isabella thought intently on the words she heard recited. "So powerful, so utterly enchanting," she thought. She felt a little warm and removed her vest. All three girls moved closer to the edge and peered through the wooden slits at the proceedings below.

"Yes...well," Father Peter mumbled. "Thank you for an interesting, uh, *example,* of your holy book. Now, let us get to the item at hand. We are taught in Christianity that God created Adam and Eve and that Eve fooled Adam into sinning. For this crime we all have inherited an evil nature which can only be forgiven when we believe in the saving blood of Jesus and in the sacraments of the church.

"We believe that Jesus is part of God, is God and will always be the Son of God. We call this divine mystery the Trinity. God the Father, God the Son and God the Holy Ghost, are all one and the same, though they have distinct personalities and persons. God the Father had to send his son to earth to die so that we may be saved. This is the basis of our beliefs in which we hold firm. Only by believing in Jesus' death on the cross can we hope to be forgiven by God and admitted to heavenly grace."

The priests and wealthy men in the audience responded with "*Amen,*" and many made the sign of the cross over their chests. Isabella felt her arms moving to do the same but then she suddenly stopped herself. It didn't feel as right anymore. Umar looking at Father Peter, appeared unfazed.

"You have explained fairly well your beliefs," Umar began, "and I commend you on the fine explanation. However, please excuse me if I say that your theories don't make any sense. If the basic principles of Christianity are the divinity of Jesus and atonement, then I think we can solve this issue with just one question: Why did God have to sacrifice a child of His in order to forgive or atone for people's sins? If a sacrifice was all that was needed, then any man or woman would have been sufficient. Why did the "son" of God have to die?"

Father Peter smiled and laughed, "Such an easy question. The son of God was needed as a sacrifice in order to forgive sins because all other people were sinful. Jesus was the only sinless man. You see, a man with sin cannot atone for other sinners. It took a perfect man."

"Okay, if you say so, but what was sacrificed, Jesus the god or Jesus the man? If Jesus the god was killed then you're saying that God, the Creator of the universe, was tortured and killed. But if the humanity of Jesus died only, then your argument falls apart because then only an ordinary man would have died, not a god."

Father Peter seemed to pause then he answered, "Our Lord Jesus was one hundred percent God and one hundred percent man at the same time. But his humanity was free from sin, so his sacrifice was necessary. No other man would have done..."

"So which part of god *died*?" Umar demanded. "If there was no human being free from sin in the world, and God had to come here Himself to be sacrificed, but His divinity did not die, then why couldn't God have just created a perfect, sinless man and then kill him for atonement?"

"God couldn't create a perfect man because of the sin of Adam..."

"Watch what you're saying, priest." Umar scolded angrily. "If Allah can create Adam sinless, then He can create any man sinless."

Father Peter appeared annoyed but continued, "God alone knows His secrets. We cannot say why He had to come here, Himself, to die for our sins. But this much we do know: His dying for us was to show how much He loved us. He even went so far as to give his only begotten son so we could have everlasting life."

"If God had such great love for His creatures, why didn't He send His son in the very beginning to be crucified? Weren't there people alive before Jesus' time who needed saving?"

"We do not know about God's mysteries," Father Peter intoned.

"My question still stands. Calling on mysteries again and again doesn't answer anything. If you say God's *humanity* died, then God's becoming a human was pointless. Some other person could have been sacrificed just as well. But if you say Jesus died, and spent three days in Hell, which I read in your Bible, then you are saying something horrible! God, or His son, *died and was punished in Hell*? *Astaghfirullah*!"

"I'm sorry, but I answered your question. You choose not to understand. Man, being sinful by nature, could never serve as a sacrifice for the ultimate atonement. Christ's humanity served the purpose because he was *innocent*."

"So," Umar shifted onto his other leg, "if I follow your reasoning, Jesus was pure, and he had to take on everyone else's sins in order to forgive them. Priest, even though I fail to understand your reasoning, I must confess that it sounds absurd. Allah teaches us that '*No one can bear the burdens of another*.' [19] It seems to me that it would have been better for this *son* of God to perform some good and righteous action which would have canceled out all the sins of man. We Muslims believe that the cure for sin is to believe in Allah, ask for His forgiveness and then to do what is morally right. Not to believe in God committing suicide to save all humanity in one shot."

"We cannot tell God what to do. He did as He liked. It is your arrogance which makes you question His motives and plan," Father Peter chided.

"What you call arrogance, we call common sense. Your own Bible, indeed, your precious Paul, states in Galatians 6:5 that, "*For every man shall bear his own burden*," retorted Umar.

---

[19] Qur'an 25:18.

"Blasphemy! You *dare* interpret the Bible you infidel!" cried Father Peter. "Only those endowed with the Holy Ghost can understand the Bible."

"Anyway," Umar resumed without a pause, "we both believe that Jesus was born from the womb of a virgin named Mary. Now, who was born, Jesus the god or Jesus the man?"

"God cannot be born, rather, it was the humanity of Jesus that was born," Father Peter droned dryly.

"So, which died on the cross, God or a man?"

Father Peter curled his eyebrow and answered, "God can never die. It was the humanity of Jesus that died."

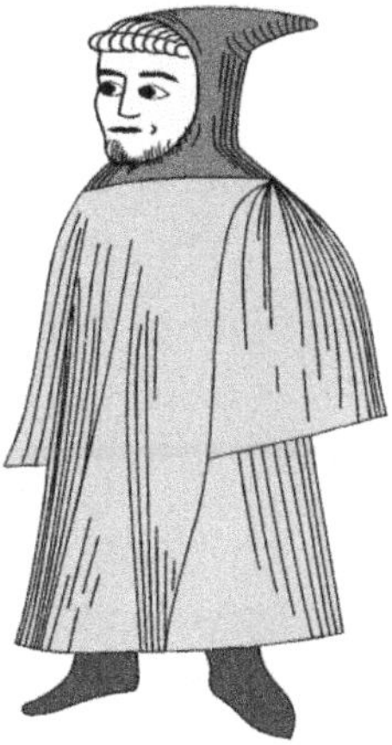

"So, the birth and supposed death of Jesus relate to his humanity and not his divinity," Umar asked.

"Yes. Certainly. Yes." Responded Peter in an uncertain voice. In the balcony above, Isabella waited tensely for what was sure to happen next.

"May I see a Bible, please?" Umar asked. Father Peter looked at the Cardinal who seemed distracted. Then he nodded his head hesitantly. Father Peter took a Bible off the table and handed it to Umar. Umar opened it up and started looking for a specific chapter.

"He can read *Latin!*" Rosa whispered to her friends. "Most Christians can't even *read!*"

"If the birth and death of Jesus related specifically to his humanity and not his divinity, then your teachings crumble like a house of cards! It says in the book of Job, chapter 14, verse 4, "*Who can bring a clean thing out of an unclean? Not one.*" So if Jesus was born of a human woman, and, being one of Adam's descendants, she was also sinful, how could a pure and innocent being have come out of an unclean being?!

"And further, in chapter 15 it infers that, "*he who is born of a woman*" is sinful and not righteous. And since, as you have agreed, that the birth of Jesus was not of divinity but was of humanity, therefore, *according to your own Bible,* even Jesus, *having been born of a woman,* was sinful! The death of his humanity could *never* atone for the sins of man!"

The three Muslims in the back stood up from their seats and shouted, "*Allahu Akbar!*" while the priests were in an uproar. Some were shouting; others were yelling. The few Christian women along the wall were wailing and crying loudly. Isabella looked at Maria and Rosa and saw the panic in their face. Strangely enough, Isabella felt calm. It was as if she expected Christianity to be crushed. She almost felt satisfied with the outcome.

"*We're ruined!*" cried Maria.

"Look at them," Rosa shouted. Down below several of the priests had rushed at Umar with fists raised. Umar, being younger and stronger easily pushed them aside and stood with his back to the wall in a crouching, wrestling stance. Several other Christians eyed him menacingly even as the Cardinal was shouting for order.

Isabella became frightened for Umar, though she didn't know why. "Watch out!" she cried as one of the men attempted to jump Umar from the side. Umar knocked him away and sent him reeling into a chair. It busted in a dozen pieces.

"Umar looked up at the balcony and saw Isabella looking down on him. He smiled wryly and waved his hand in gratitude. By that time, Sheikh Samir and the two merchants reached him and formed a defensive perimeter. The Muslim sister had pulled out a small dagger from somewhere and stood ready.

The Cardinal's shouts finally started having some effect as the angry priests and other Christians moved back.

"I'm afraid I must ask you to leave this house immediately!" the Cardinal demanded. "And you can be sure that we will report this violence of yours to the Ministry of *Dhimmis'*." [20]

"Yes," responded the Sheikh. "I'd like for you to do that. Then it can be made public what Christians do when you prove their beliefs wrong!"

The Cardinal just glared at him and motioned towards the door. The crowd moved back, leaving an

---

[20] A *dhimmi* is a non-Muslim living under the protection of the Muslim state. They pay a special tax called the jizyah and this entitles them to avoid having to serve in the army and also helps cover the costs of Muslim-non-Muslim relations. Every Islamic government has a special department to make sure that justice is done in affairs between Muslims and non-Muslims. In Islam, everyone has basic rights no matter what religion they are.

open path to the main door. As the four Muslims walked out, Umar looked up at Isabella again and she returned his glance. She smiled at him and watched him leave.

6

A Private Quest

Isabella lay on her bed long past daybreak. A slight breeze danced through the curtains and cooled her worried brow. What did it all mean? Sure, the Muslims were more powerful when it came to fighting, but Christians had always taken comfort in believing that their religion would eventually convert them over. But now Isabella saw that Islam might have more truth to it than her father's religion.

After the meeting at Father Peter's house, it looked as if Christianity was a bunch of unanswerable questions that made no sense. Was Jesus really God? The Bible itself seemed to be very evasive on this issue. Couldn't God forgive people, like Umar said, without killing his own son? And what about those beautiful passages from the Qur'an Umar had read? Isabella felt like her head was a wreck. "What do I believe?" She whispered softly.

She took her Bible off the night stand and thumbed through its pages. She felt as if she was looking at it for the first time. Occasionally, she would stop to read a passage here and there. She saw page after page of laws in the Old Testament. But when she flipped through the New Testament, she saw in Paul's writings laws after laws as well.

Some of the laws began to make her angry. When she read the Bible in the past, she always glossed over anything she didn't agree with, after all, Jesus was more important than a few words on a page. But as she read passage after passage, she realized that most of the Bible sounded like people's opinions rather than revelation.

She read I Timothy, verse 4 which said, *"Neither give heed to fables and endless genealogies which minister questions."* But then she realized that there were endless genealogies (family trees) all over the Old and New Testament! Then she read in the same book in chapter 2, verses 11-15, *"Let the woman learn in silence with all subjection. But I suffer not a woman to teach, nor to take authority over the man, but to be in silence. For Adam was first formed, then Eve. And Adam was not deceived, but the woman being deceived was in the transgression."*

"What?" Isabella shouted. *"That's not fair.* Women have to be *silent*! They can't teach men! Adam wasn't wrong, but Eve was?" She felt as if her eyes opened for the first time. "I've seen plenty of Muslim women teaching men in the state-run colleges. If they let their women teach men, why can't we?" She hadn't realized before how anti-woman the Bible was.

But while she began to doubt the Bible as revelation, she had nothing to replace it in her heart and mind.

"What's the Qur'an like?" She mused. She had never seen one before and as far as she knew, it was only in Arabic, a language she couldn't understand.

She remembered how Father Peter had tried to use information from the Qur'an during the first meeting to trip Umar up. But it didn't work. Umar was just too smart for such tricks. The only time she ever heard what the Qur'an said was yesterday when he read those beautiful verses telling how God doesn't have any equals. She felt a rush of heat and became restless. She wanted to read that book. She had to know what it said, but how?

After spending a few more hours in her room, Isabella heard a knock at her door. She recognized it as the maidservant. "Come in," she said.

Quickly, the maidservant opened the door and said, "Mistress, your father would like to see you right away."

"I'll be there in a few minutes." She replied.

"No," insisted the maidservant. "Your father wants to see you *right now*."

"Okay, I'm coming." She responded as she quickly dressed and washed her face.

When she reached her father in his dimly-lit study, he was sitting in his usual leather-bound chair. He seemed somehow disturbed. "Isabella," he said. "Come in my child."

She walked into the room and stood before him, head slightly bowed. What this was all about she had no clue.

"I've been thinking lately," he began. "Thinking that it's time to do the best action I could ever do. You know, I never expected to have a child. I felt from an early age the call of following Christ. It was quite a fluke, actually, which caused me to marry your mother so long ago. And after she died, I took that as a sign to give up worldly occupations and to dedicate my life to the church. In that, your friend Maria's father and myself are similar.

"The reason I entered the priesthood right away was so that I wouldn't feel lonely and be tempted to marry again. Since then, I studied with great zeal and have followed the church's prohibition about priests being married to the letter. Now, I'm telling you this so you can understand that true satisfaction comes from serving the Lord and not from the pleasures of the flesh."

Her father paused a moment. He leaned forward slowly. Isabella noticed his eyes narrow and glint in the dim light. He looked scary. "I saw you warn that *Mozzlem*, Umar, and I also saw how he looked at you." He hissed.

Isabella opened her mouth to protest, but a raised hand from her father silenced her.

"Now," he continued. "I think it's time to do what I've been planning for so long. This is the best thing for you as it will save you from the temptations of the flesh. It's already been decided and arranged. I'm sending you to the convent next month to begin your training as a nun."

Isabella almost fainted from loss of breath. Her head spun, and her knees felt weak. She caught the edge of a table with her hands and leaned on it heavily.

"You know it's the best thing, my Isabella," intoned her father. "And I won't have you marrying a *Mozzlem*, or anyone at all for that matter. You are my daughter, and you will follow the example of the Virgin Mary. Nuns are married to Jesus Christ, and he will be the best husband you could ever hope to have!"

Isabella whirled around and ran from the room as fast as she could. She stomped up the stairs and nearly knocked over the maidservant who was carrying a basket downstairs. She could barely hold the tears back and she felt her belly twist in knots. She slammed the door to her room shut and threw herself on the bed, sobbing and crying.

A little while later she sat upright, clutching her pillow close to her chest. Her eyes were raw from the tears, and her hair was all in tangles. Her Bible lay open on her night stand. She picked it up and held it before her. She opened it at random and began to read first Corinthians, 13:11. It said:

"But when I was a child, I spoke as a child, I understood as a child, I thought as a child; but when I became a man, I put

away childish things. For now, we see through a glass, darkly; but then face to face..."

Though the words were wise, she finally knew: this was not revelation from God, but the thoughts, musings and feelings of many ordinary men. She was a child before, she knew, now it was time to grow up. Now it was time to meet her challenge *face to face*.

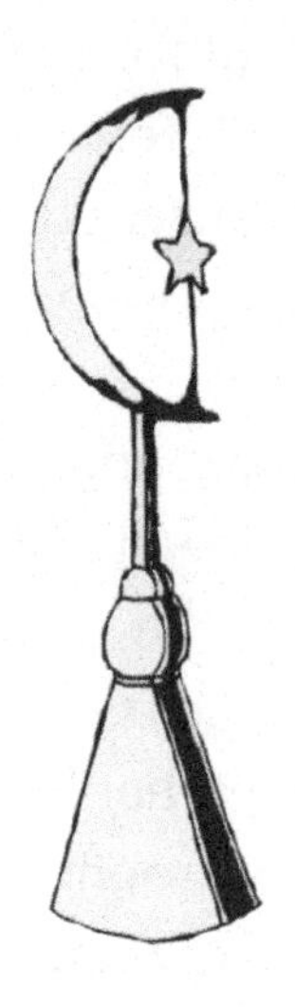

7

Face to Face

A faint breeze rustled through the trees overhead causing a few leaves to fall earthward. The morning sun was just beginning its climb through the sky and the misty dew clung to its last hidden alcoves. "*Alhumdulillah,*" spoke a voice so faint that it passed away almost unnoticed by the other being present.

"Yes." Sheikh Samir answered. "It *is* a beautiful morning, Umar."

The two men had walked to the *Janaina* garden after the morning prayer, as was their custom, and were enjoying the crisp, new air which could only be found amid trees and flowers as they awoke from their dreamy sleep.

"I heard of several Christians who reverted [21] to Islam yesterday," the Sheikh said. "I even personally took the *shahadah* [22] of an old man myself."

"It is Allah who plants guidance into any heart willing to receive it." replied Umar.

---

[21] Reverted literally means to accept Islam.
[22] Declaration of becoming a Muslim.

"Imagine that, one Christian girl arranges a dialogue and Christianity itself is on the run."

"Indeed." Umar replied thoughtfully. "I wonder about her. I guess she's the Cardinal's daughter. He can't be too happy with her actions I suppose."

"Why do you think she warned you when those men were attacking you in that priest's house?" the Sheikh asked.

"I don't know, really, but I..."

Just then, the two men were interrupted by the sound of footsteps drawing near. A moment later they were surprised to see a young woman approaching them. It was the same one whom they were just discussing! She stopped a few feet in front of the men and looked at them both.

"Please excuse the intrusion." She began. "I would like to talk with you if I may."

Sheikh Samir and Umar looked at each other and then the Sheikh answered, "By all means. Here, sit down on the bench. We will stand."

Umar and the Sheikh began to get up, but she waved her arms in front of her, "No, please. I want to stand."

The two men exchanged glances again and then settled themselves back down. Isabella adjusted her vest by habit and then began to speak.

"I... I don't know where to begin," she stammered. "I'm afraid I don't know much about your religion. But after seeing how you," she looked at Umar, "were able to so easily put down Christianity, I guess I've been...well, thinking a lot about that."

"Our intention was not to put down your beliefs my dear child." The Sheikh said kindly. "We had to be a little forceful about it, though, because of the kind of close-mindedness we were up against. Our book, the Holy Qur'an, teaches us that we should reason with people in good and respectful ways. If we fell short a little bit, it is because of our own weaknesses."

"Yes," she laughed slightly. "I know the priests *were a little rough.*"

"I'll say," Umar exclaimed. "I almost had the *faith* knocked right out of me!"

The three laughed and the light discussion made Isabella feel a little less nervous. She felt as if she could proceed with this after all.

"There's a couple of benches facing each other around the corner." the Sheikh announced. "I think it may be more comfortable for talking if we were all seated."

"Yes," Isabella answered. "Let's go."

Slowly, the three walked past beautiful flower gardens, each commenting on the wonderful colors and fragrance they noticed, until they reached the two benches that were very close to each other. The two men sat on one bench while Isabella sat on the facing one.

"I wanted you to know that I meant no harm when I asked you to meet with the priests." Isabella said to Umar.

"No harm was done," he responded, smiling. "I was thankful for the experience of confronting church leaders and seeing for myself how they would handle the issues. I dare say I found myself rather enjoying it."

"Where did you learn all those things about the Bible? Father Peter knew some things about the Qur'an, but you proved his points wrong also. You clearly had the advantage in knowing about both books."

"We are taught by Allah to investigate everything we don't know about. That's why, for example, our government is building so many new colleges all over the country. I wanted to learn something, and I studied it. It's not hard, after all, to find problems with the man-made Bible."

"Indeed," Isabella responded under her breath, remembering the negative things she noticed for the first time in her latest Bible reading sessions. "That's for sure. Who was that lady who was with you? I thought Muslim women had to stay home."

Sheikh Samir laughed, "Stay home? Muslim women? Hardly. That was sister Khadija. She's an administrator in the department of the Treasury, a part-time teacher and she's a *Hafizah* besides."

"What's a *Hafizah?*" asked Isabella.

"It's a woman who has memorized the whole Qur'an." responded Umar.

"Does she teach only *Muslim* women?"

"No. She teaches an evening class on Qur'anic law in the university. She has both male and female students," answered the Sheikh.

She looked down for a minute and then raised her head again. Sheikh Samir noted the look on her face and asked, "You aren't fully sure about the truth of Christian beliefs, are you?"

For a moment she seemed to be suspended in time. She had never wanted to confront the issue so abruptly or openly. It *was* what she was feeling, but how to face it? She grew up in the church. Her father was a Cardinal! She saw an image of the priests attacking Umar after he bested them and lost all hesitation.

"Yes," she said. "After hearing the verses from the Qur'an, I thought I would like to read that book. I've opened my eyes, I feel, to what the Bible really is about, and I don't feel satisfied with it. It doesn't *speak to me* the way those Qur'an verses did."

"I've found the same thing in my study of both books," Umar agreed. "The Bible is more like a jumble of different people's opinions and stories, whereas the Qur'an is like a continuous dialogue to humans from their Creator. The difference is astounding."

"I wish I could read the Qur'an, but I don't know Arabic. Are there any translations?" Isabella asked hopefully.

"Not of the whole book," responded the Sheikh. "I'm afraid no one has done a complete translation in the Spanish language. The problem is that Allah used the best form of the Arabic language to convey His message. Even the Arabs marvel at how perfect the language used is. It's hard to translate perfection. So much meaning, emotion and fervor is lost. That's why Muslims everywhere learn Qur'anic Arabic- so they can read the revelation in its best and most perfect form. Exactly as it was revealed to the Blessed Prophet Muhammad."

"I'm from Sicily, and I learned Arabic, though it took a while," Umar recounted. "When I read the revelation, sometimes I want to cry. It's so beautiful."

"And I'm originally from Persia," added the Sheikh. "But I knew that I wanted Allah's words to speak to me, to my heart, in the language He used to speak to people for the last time."

"I've heard of Muhammad," Isabella said. "But my tutors always told me that he was a liar, that he copied the Bible and that he killed people."

"Of course, these are the stories people will make up when they're afraid of the other side," the Sheikh answered. "In reality, the Blessed Prophet, may peace be upon him, was known for his truthfulness and excellent manner. Can you believe it? He didn't know how to read or write, yet Allah chose him for the revelation! He could never have copied the Bible because there *were no* Bibles in the Arabic language, and he couldn't have read one anyway. And I think you'll agree that after hearing some verses from the Qur'an being recited, that the Qur'an is nothing like the Bible at all in style, tone or structure."

Isabella nodded her head in agreement. It was true. She knew instinctively that the two books were completely different.

"And as for Muhammad, peace be upon him, harming people," Umar intoned, "if you'll learn about his life, he always forgave those who hurt him and spared the lives of those who tried to *kill him.* The Qur'an commands us, *'La ikraha fi deen'* - 'There is no forcing anyone into this way of life.' [23] What this means is that no one can be forced to become a Muslim. Everyone must listen to their heart and decide when the time is right. Do you see Muslims

[23] Qur'an 2:256.

forcing the Christians of this land to convert? No. Our government has controlled Spain for almost two hundred years now and still many people remain Christians of their own free will."

Isabella realized the truth of his words. Christianity was allowed to flourish even though the country was ruled by Muslims. Suddenly, everything her tutor said that was negative about Islam looked transparent and left her thoughts. She decided she would learn for herself first hand before making judgments about others.

"What does Islam teach, Reverend Father?" she asked Sheikh Samir. "I don't really know."

"Well," the Sheikh began, "first of all, Islam teaches that only Allah is revered. No man or woman is special or holy in themselves. So just call me Brother Samir or Sheikh Samir if you prefer. The word Sheikh just means I went to school and learned a lot. It's not a title or office like the way being a priest is supposed to be *holy.*"

Isabella agreed, but she felt a little weird thinking that she was the equal of this older man. The Sheikh continued, "We believe that Allah, God, is one, with no partners or sons. He is not a male or female nor is He divided up into parts, like Christianity teaches."

"I was always taught that God was a male. The book of Genesis says that God created man in his own image, the likeness of a man," Isabella said.

"Nobody knows who wrote those words," the Sheikh answered. "So many people wrote their own ideas and stories, and one day somebody gathered a bunch of this stuff together and called it their holy book. I saw a translated Greek book that said the Bible was put together in the year 325 - *by a vote!* That's 300 years after the time of Prophet Jesus!

"Allah's revelation, by contrast, came complete in the lifetime of His last Prophet. To this day nobody has changed a word, and nobody ever will. So take what I'm saying as something that is organized and consistent. The Bible also says that Adam did not sin, but Eve did. Does that sound like a man's opinion or what?"

"I know." responded Isabella. "Please, continue."

"Next, we believe that Allah has made people to be sort of like caretakers on earth. He gave us a free-will and lets us choose for our own selves how we will behave. He gave us an inner sense of right and wrong to help us make good choices. At the same time, we can be weak in the face of temptation and may fall into sinful ways.

"To help guide us further, Allah sent prophets to different communities to teach the people Allah's laws for them. Those who followed them prospered while those who disobeyed them brought ruin on themselves. Jesus, for example, was the last Prophet Allah sent to the Jews. He was no *son of god* or *god on earth* walking around and eating bread."

Umar and Isabella laughed heartily at the remark. For the first time since all of this began, Isabella began to feel at ease. She felt older, somehow, as if she was no longer the young girl who liked to gossip and wander around. The conversation continued on well past noon. She asked so many questions and received answers that she could understand. Not once was the word, *mystery,* mentioned. She liked that.

The call for the mid-day prayer stole softly over the wind like a silver leaf in flight. Sheikh Samir, Umar and Isabella listened to it in silence. When it was over, Isabella felt a tugging at her heart. She wanted to follow the call of that voice. She thought she had better not ask, however, for she might appear impetuous.

"Sheikh Samir," Umar said. "Do you think there would be any problem if we asked our new friend here to accompany us to the Masjid?"

The Sheikh smiled, "No, I see no problem at all. That is, if she would like to come."

"Oh no, I couldn't," she protested. "It wouldn't be proper for me to go, being a Christian and the daughter of a cardinal and all..."

"But I believe in your heart you are already a daughter of Islam, my child," the Sheikh answered softly.

"I don't know," she said fleetingly. "I feel something. I mean, I like what I've learned. It's *just* - well, my father is who he is and I... I'm just so *confused*."

"Pray to God for guidance," Umar implored. "When the time is right, He can guide you to what is best for you. Allah never turns down a request for guidance from a sincere seeker of truth."

"Yes," she answered. "I'll do that. I'll pray to be shown the right way. Can we meet here again, at the same time?"

"I think so," the Sheikh said. "Tomorrow I have to lecture at the main college, but the day after would be fine."

"And I have some business to attend to tomorrow as well," Umar added. "One of my Christian associates invited me to view some new trade goods he just received. But I'm free the next day as well."

"Then it's agreed," the Sheikh announced. "Two days hence we will meet here again to continue our discussions."

"I look forward to it." Isabella said as she stood from her seat.

The two men stood likewise, and the three parted from each other. Isabella thought about turning around and following the men to the Mosque, but then thought she had better think some more.

She walked a little lighter and a little easier than when she first left her home. *"Allah,"* she said quietly, purposefully using the Arabic name for God, *"guide me to the right way."*

8

Trouble at Home

Early the next morning Isabella was awakened by the sounds of the call to prayer. It was still dark out, and all was still in the house. How beautiful it seemed to her. Although she had heard the adhan all her life, given that Muslims were in charge, still, she had never paid much attention to it. She rolled over in her bed and stared out the window. The drowsiness in her eyes made her feel as if she were floating along the clouds, chasing after the words...*'Hayya alasalah...Hayyah alal falah....' - 'Come to prayer...Come to success.'*

She knew that Muslims would be getting up and making their way to the Mosque for prayer. How glorious, she thought, to pray to God before the rest of the world awoke. By contrast, she knew that her fellow Christians were still fast asleep and dreaming in their warm covers.

She could stand it no longer. She got out of bed and put on her night gown. She washed her face and hands and feet. She didn't know exactly how the Muslims washed for prayer, but this would have to do. When she was finished, she went to a corner of her room and lowered herself to her knees.

She paused for a moment and then bowed her head to the floor. "Please, *Allah*," she prayed, "show me the straight way. Guide me to the right, and help me understand what I should do."

She bowed and prayed for half an hour until she felt sleepy. Then, she returned to her bed and dreamed pleasantly until the sun was long past risen.

When she awoke again, it was nearly noon. She rarely slept this late and felt a little ashamed. She thought about what she had done after hearing the morning adhan. It didn't seem at all strange to her. She sort of felt whole and alive. It felt good to place her head on the floor, to totally bow one's heart and body to God. She scratched her head and wondered what the day would hold.

After a quick bath, she dressed herself and went downstairs for breakfast. Her father wasn't in his study, so she entered the kitchen and ate alone, seeing no one. Out of nowhere she remembered what had happened at Maria's house when the second meeting was being held.

Friar Michael, her beloved tutor, had whispered something to Father Peter and her father, the Cardinal. What they whispered back made him angry and upset. What did they tell him? She had to know. So, she resolved to visit him today and ask him what happened.

When breakfast was finished, she grabbed her handbag and scurried out the door as fast as she could. But before she could leave the courtyard, she stopped in her tracks. Standing in front of the main gate was her father, wearing all his black priestly robes. A huge crucifix hung from a chain around his neck, and a Bible was in his left hand.

"Isabella!" he demanded. "Go to my study!" He scowled as he addressed her. She had never seen his face look so angry and disfigured. She felt her heart skip a beat and a great emptiness open up in her belly. She felt sick and turned as fast as she could to obey his strange command.

He followed her into the study, saying not a word. Once inside, he closed the door and locked it. Something wasn't right, and Isabella knew it.

Her father pushed her into his leather chair and stood over her, glaring. She sank back trying to burrow into the cushions. What was happening!

"Do you have anything to tell me?" he demanded.

Isabella remained silent and bowed her head in fear. She lost feeling in her arms and legs.

"Speak up child!" he yelled. "This is your chance to confess."

"I did confession last week with Friar Michael," she answered meekly. "He pardoned all my sins already." [24]

"Oh, but I think you have committed fresh sins, horrible sins since then!" he bellowed. "I know you've been seeing that filthy *Mozzlem*! Don't think I don't have people who inform me. Have you accepted his lies? Did you convert to his beliefs?"

Isabella cowered in fear. She had never seen her father like this before. He was raging; his face was disfigured by sweat and tension. His hands were clenched in tight fists.

"Speak now, girl!" he cried. "Or by Christ Jesus I'll beat the truth out of you!"

"I have not yet accepted Islam, but I am still a Christian," she whispered.

"Does this mean that you're going to accept it in the future?" he demanded.

---

[24] The Catholic Church teaches that everyone must go to a priest and tell them all the sins and bad things they did or thought that week. The priest then forgives them their sins and gives them some type of work to do as punishment. This is called confession.

"Why are you asking me about the future?" she felt emboldened. "I could ask you the same question."

"What do you think about Islam, then?"

Isabella sat a little straighter and replied, "I don't hate Islam like I was taught to. I find a lot of good in it and many things similar to our own beliefs. I..."

"Enough!" her father shouted. "I knew something like this would happen! You have been tempted by the flesh! That infidel Umar has beguiled your heart and clouded your reasoning!"

"That's not true!" she protested. "He is an honorable man, and my feelings about Islam have not been influenced by him in the least."

"Liar!" he screamed, as he slapped her across the face. The sudden stinging cold startled her into silence. A moment later tears of pain mixed with the anger of betrayal ran down her face.

"You've been living for too long as a foolish young girl," he said loudly, pointing his finger absently in the air and pacing back and forth. "I will not have all my years of dedication and hard work in raising you to be righteous simply vanish in the lusts of the flesh. I've spoken to my associates and have arranged for you to be taken to the convent tomorrow."

Isabella looked up at him in horror.

"There," he intoned, stopping to turn towards her, you will be shielded from temptations and will learn to accept the truth of our Lord Jesus Christ.

Until you depart, you are to remain in the house and are not allowed to leave."

With that said, he stepped back towards the door and opened it. With his figure outlined by the light from outside he looked like an evil demon sent to torment her. He didn't seem like her father anymore. Before leaving he laughed cruelly and said, "By the way, you won't have to worry about being tempted by that *Umar* any longer. I've taken *care of him*."

He closed the door. Isabella was left with silence. She sat there stunned for a time. The odor of the chair invaded her nostrils and nauseated her. Her world was turned upside down. The sharp pain on her cheek hurt but not more than the wound in her heart. She knew that for her, her father was dead, his beliefs were dead and most of all, her faith in a man-god was over.

9

Last Hope

Isabella spent the rest of the day in her room. Her father had posted a guard at the front gate, so there was no hope of escape. Her meals were brought to her by her maidservant, though she didn't feel hungry. All she could think about was what happened earlier in the day.

Her father, the Cardinal, was considered a devoted man and priest. How could he abuse her and accuse her of what she was not even guilty of? He was going to send her to the convent the next day. How could she go? Up until then, it was always something that was far off in the future. Now she was facing it with no way out.

She heard about what happens at the convents. The monks and priests come periodically to satisfy their lusts on the nuns. "Vow of chastity my foot!" she stammered. "The church forbids priests and nuns from marrying, yet then they engage in the worst secret behavior."

She knew she didn't want to go.

That evening, the maidservant came and packed some of Isabella's things. Isabella watched in silence as the maidservant pushed aside her favorite dresses and chose only a few drab looking outfits. "I guess nuns don't believe in nice clothes," she muttered.

The maidservant merely looked at her and said, "I'm only doing what I'm told. At the convent you'll need nothing but yourself and a few small things. Your days of fine dresses, seeing friends and long walks through the city are over."

Isabella slumped over onto her bed heavily. When the maidservant finished, she left quietly and closed the door behind her. There in the corner stood two small bags. Looking around the room, Isabella noticed all the things she had to leave behind: her beautiful clothes, shoes and ribbons. None of her books had been packed except the Bible. Her combs and jewelry hadn't been touched.

She threw herself back against her pillows and couldn't decide whether to cry or yell in anger. This wasn't happening to her! Frantically, she thought about what to do. She had to escape. She had no choice but to run away. But where would she go, she thought. One name came to mind: Friar Michael. He would help her somehow. He had to!

There wasn't much time. She had to be ready to make her escape. As quickly as she could, she dug a large bag out of the closet. In it she put her jewelry, combs, two favorite dresses and some extra shoes. She also took a bed sheet and stuffed it inside leaving the bag quite full. Next, she laid out the set of clothes she would wear during her escape and found a few coins in the bottom of her dresser drawer. You never know when money would come in handy.

All the activity made her feel better, but it also distracted her from how she was going to get out of her house. When she finished her preparations, she realized that one obstacle lay in her way yet: the guard at the door. He had orders not to let Isabella out, and there was no other exit from the house. When she realized the difficulty she faced, she sat on the bed and stared blankly.

She could never hope to fight a grown man or outrun him. It all seemed so hopeless. Her heart sank and she stomped in anger. "Allah," she said earnestly, "find me a way out."

A few moments passed, and her heart sank further. There would be no way out. But just then, something miraculous, for so it seemed to her, happened. Faintly, carried over the breeze like angels' wings, the words of the *adhan* crept softly into her room. The Muslims were being called to their night prayer. *"That's it!"* She exclaimed. She knew what she would do.

She immediately went to the wash bowl to clean herself for prayer. After she did the best she could, she went to her usual spot and dropped to her knees to pray. She had never prayed so hard in all her life. After nearly half an hour of bowing and asking Allah's help, she went to bed.

As she wished, she was awakened to the sounds of the *adhan* in the early morning. It was still dark out and most people would be fast asleep. "Not so, the Muslims," she thought proudly. She quickly dressed herself, washed up, grabbed her bags and made ready to leave. After taking one last look around at her old room, knowing she would probably never see it again, she silently shut the door and crept down the stairs.

Everything in the house was still. Even the maidservant was not yet up. When she reached the front door, she carefully turned the lock and swung it open slowly. It made a small squeaking noise that might as well have been alarm bells to Isabella. No one came. There were no shouts of "catch her!" So far, so good.

After closing the door as haltingly as she could, she tip-toed across the courtyard towards the front gate. In the dim light of first dawn she could make out the form of the guard. He was slumped up against the wall, snoring. *"Thank you, Allah."* She thought. She slipped away into the night in the direction of Friar Michael's home.

10
Friar Michael

"Who can it be *at this hour?*" A groggy Friar Michael wondered. The knocking on his door was loud and sounded urgent. He slowly rolled himself out of bed and, after donning a robe, went to answer the strange early morning summons.

When he opened the door, he was surprised to see Isabella standing there with a bag in her hand and a hood draped over her head. "Bless me Lord! What are you doing here at this hour, my child?"

"Please, Friar Michael, may I come in? It's urgent."

The rotund Friar moved aside and waved her inside. After taking her bag and cloak from her, he ushered her into his small sitting room. "Now, my dear," he began. "What seems to be the trouble, and does your father know you're here?"

"No." She responded. "My father doesn't know I'm here, and he must not find out either."

"*Hhhmm, I see.* What sort of trouble have you gotten into?"

"Yesterday, my father hit me and is now forcing me to go to the convent. I had to run away; I couldn't stay. He accused me of being an unfaithful daughter and an infidel."

"Have you been unfaithful?"

"No, most certainly not!"

"Are you an infidel?"

"I don't know. I don't know if I am or not. I have serious doubts about Christian teachings and have found much to admire in the Islamic faith. I think I'm inclined to accept Islam. For that my father went nearly insane. I've never seen him that way before."

"Blessings, may the Lord forgive," intoned the Friar. "I don't claim to understand all the mysteries of the Christian religion, but then again, I don't question the will of the Almighty. I respect your doubts and the choice you are moving towards. We all seek the truth, and let him who finds it rejoice. Now, what would you like me to do?"

"I don't know. I guess I need a place to stay or somewhere to go. I could never go to the convent now. It would kill me."

"Or they would kill you," Friar Michael lamented.

"What do you mean?"

"Well, I'm not supposed to discuss the subject, but given that it may directly affect you, I believe you have a right to know. The local parish has been concerned about the number of Christians who have accepted Islam of late. To stop this they've called in the Order of the Inquisition."

"Order of Inquisition? What's that?" Asked Isabella.

"It's a secret group of priests and sympathizers who identify weak Christians who may be thinking about Islam. They kidnap them and take them to a secret location where they are forced, and sometimes tortured, into confessing their sins and reaffirming their allegiance to the Pope in Rome. [25]

"Just the mere threat of being taken by the Order keeps people from converting. If they found out about you, then you would suffer a horrible fate."

"I've never heard of the Order before. If my father found out about it he would shut it..."

"Your father," Friar Michael interrupted, *"is a leading member of the Order."*

Isabella froze in horror. Her father, a member of a secret society! One that kidnaps and tortures people! She would have never believed it before, but after seeing a side of her father she never knew existed, now it seemed more plausible.

Just then a terrible thought came to her mind. Umar! Didn't her father say that she wouldn't ever

[25] The Pope is the holy leader of all Catholics. He is supposed to be sinless and never wrong.

have to think about him again? Didn't he say that he *took care* of him?

"Oh my God!" she cried.

"What is it?" Friar Michael asked.

"Something my father said yesterday. He said he *took care* of Umar, so I could never think about him again. Do you think they did something to him? Is he in any danger?"

"I believe so, my young Isabella," he responded gravely. "At the last meeting in Father Peter's house, your father whispered to me that if this Umar wouldn't convert to Christianity, then he would be taken by the Order and made to convert so as to shame the Muslims."

"That's why you appeared so upset!" Isabella resounded. "I could see your expression from the balcony. But if they have Umar, won't the Muslim government send soldiers to rescue him?"

"The Muslim authorities don't know about the Order, or its secret location. Besides, if a hundred men on horseback came charging over the hill, they would kill Umar and dispose of his body before the soldiers could ever find him."

"We must do something. Every minute they have him he is in mortal danger!" cried Isabella.

"Do you really care for him, my child?" he asked tenderly.

"I…uh...well," she stammered, but then, gaining confidence, she stated, "Yes!"

"Then I will help you. Let's decide on a plan."

The pair talked until the sun had risen well over the horizon. Finally, with their course of action clear, the pair set out towards the *Janaina* garden. Isabella was extra careful to hold her hood over her head.

11
The Plot

Alone on a bench sat Sheikh Samir. He had been waiting for his friend, Umar for over an hour. Isabella, with whom they had a meeting planned, was also late. "Allah is with the patient." He reminded himself and looked around at the beauties and delights of the garden. He could wait here.

A few minutes later he heard two sets of footsteps approaching from around the corner. But it was not entirely who he expected. Isabella came and stood before him, accompanied by a large, round Christian Friar. "*Greetings,*" the Friar announced.

"And the same to you," the Sheikh responded. "I didn't realize you were going to bring one of your priests with you to talk. But that's fine with me. I'm afraid, however, that Umar has not yet arrived. He was at the Masjid for Fajr prayer but after that I didn't see him."

"Did he say where he was going?" asked the Friar.

"Well, he said he had to go to a Christian associate of his to see some trade goods. But that shouldn't have taken very long."

Isabella looked at Friar Michael worriedly.

Friar Michael turned to the Sheikh and said, "Your friend is in great danger. A secret Christian group called the Order of the Inquisition has probably kidnapped him and is holding him prisoner."

"But why?" asked the Sheikh in astonishment.

"Because he embarrassed the Christian religion publicly and also because," he looked at Isabella, "he may have gotten a bit too close with the daughter of the Cardinal. For that, she is in danger as well"

"I see," replied the Sheikh carefully. "I must go at once to inform the authorities." As he began to rise, Friar Michael leaned forward and implored, "Please wait, listen to what I must tell you."

The Sheikh paused and then nodded.

"If your soldiers try to rescue him, he's a dead man. It must be done another way."

"Allah is a witness over all that men do," he sighed. "I'm listening."

Friar Michael proceeded to tell the Sheikh the plan that he and Isabella came up with. When he had finished, the Sheikh reluctantly agreed, but on the condition that if their attempt failed, he would be allowed to go to the authorities at once. For this purpose, the Friar had to tell the Sheikh the secret location of the Order.

It was agreed, and the Sheikh left on some important business he said he had to do. Isabella watched him leave and asked, "Do you think he'll keep his word and not go straight to the soldiers? After all, he knows where the Order's hideout is now."

"I believe he is a man of truth." The Friar answered. With that said, Isabella followed the Friar to his home for some last-minute preparations. They would slip out of the city's walls soon thereafter.

12

The Quest

The afternoon sun hung low in the sky over two lone horsemen. Through grassy plains and over gently rolling hills they rode at breakneck speed. Mile after mile passed as the pair entered ever more remote regions. The quicker of the two sometimes had to slow her steed in order to let the over burdened horse of her companion to catch up. On these horses rode Isabella and Friar Michael to a place only the Friar was familiar with.

After three hours of steady riding, the Friar motioned for them to halt. The foamy sweat of the horse's mane glistened in the waning light. Isabella had been taught to ride a horse when she was younger, but she never dreamed she would be racing into the countryside to save a man that weeks before she would have considered an enemy. But the beliefs that would have produced those feelings were gone now, and new ones were taking their place. First and foremost was the belief that Umar needed to be safe.

The Friar stumbled off his tired horse, nearly knocking it over with his weight in the process while Isabella jumped off hers gracefully. "We're very close now," the Friar puffed, trying to catch his breath.

"I'm ready," Isabella answered.

She followed Friar Michael, leading the horses by their straps until they came to a small thicket of trees. They tied their horses to a bush, and Isabella loosened a bundle off of hers and carried it off into the forest a little way.

When she returned, after some minutes, she resembled the smitten image of a nun from the convent, or so thought the Friar.

"Bless me, Jesus!" he exclaimed. "It's a shame you don't wish to be a nun, for you look like the Virgin Mary herself."

"Strange," Isabella muttered. "I've heard *that* before."

The pair set off through the thick forest underbrush. Several ruined structures cast an air of foreboding over the misty evening air.

"Those are the ruins of guard towers from the last war," the Friar remarked. "Some say this place is haunted. That's why people stay away from this area."

"The perfect place for a hide-out," Isabella replied.

They continued on through the trees until they emerged on the other side of a dense thicket. Across the valley ahead of them stood an old, stone monastery. It was elevated on a barren hill and looked like an imposing, dark place from where they were standing.

"He's in there?" Isabella asked. "That place looks like it hasn't been lived in for years."

"Looks can be deceiving, my child," Friar Michael returned. "The Order wants passersby to think the monastery is ruined and abandoned, especially the Muslims, who have a dislike for going into ruins." [26]

"There's the entrance over there, I think," Isabella announced as she pointed to a huge cavernous opening near the front of the building.

"That's the way in for fools," exclaimed the Friar. "You would find nothing but a few moldy rooms and rats inside. The real entrance is behind the building, and that one leads underground, where the Order does its business."

---

[26] Islam teaches that old ruins are a sign to show the living that all people will pass away some day, and therefore they should take a warning from the demise of the people of the past.

Isabella felt a shiver down her spine and wondered what she was doing. But she knew what was at stake and followed the Friar as he carefully made his way along the edge of the valley towards the rear side of the old monastery. They stopped to rest for a few moments behind a stand of trees, then they moved on again.

Once they reached the rear of the valley, they crouched down behind some rocks to get a closer look at the secret entrance. The sun was almost gone from the sky and the twilight was just around the corner. From where they were hiding, they could make out two small torches next to a small, rotting door.

"There are two guards there. Each one holds a torch. See their shadows on the wall behind them?"

Isabella squinted her eyes and nodded silently.

"Listen carefully, Isabella, I have a plan for getting in."

After the Friar explained himself to her, they both set off in different directions toward the entrance. Isabella walked straight towards the guards.

"What a lousy night!" one guard said to the other.

"I'm sick of always doing guard duty while the other guys get to stay inside where all the action is!" replied the other.

"Maybe we should take this up with some of the..."

Suddenly, a small figure stepped out of the shadows in front of them.

"Who goes there?" demanded one of the guards as he extended his torch towards the unknown person. The other guard unsheathed his sword and stood ready.

"I'm a humble nun from the convent," the person whispered back. "I have come to *relieve* your boredom."

"Well," the second guard exclaimed gleefully, "that's more like it." He sheathed his sword and moved closer to the fragile young woman. Just as he was about to lay his hands on her, a loud bellow boomed out from above and the two guards looked up in time to see a huge, fat man falling right on top of them. They were crushed unconscious instantly.

"They'll be out for a while, I think," huffed Friar Michael as he struggled to get off the limp bodies of the guards.

"I should think at least *a week*," resounded Isabella cheerfully. "Now, let's go," she beckoned them forward.

The Friar picked up one of the torches and pushed into the darkness ahead. Isabella took a deep breath, and followed him into the secret entrance.

13

The Order of the Inquisition

The passageway was narrow and low which made the going slow at first. The smell of dank, putrid air hung about the rotted timbers like mist in the morning. Slowly, they moved on down the winding hall until they noticed that it began to descend steeply. "We're going deeper under the monastery," commented Friar Michael.

"How far down is this place?" inquired Isabella.

"These passages are ancient. They go on for about half a mile or more."

"Wow!" she exclaimed. "This is a regular endless maze. I'm glad we brought a torch along."

"It won't last long. We have to get to the main chamber before we lose our light."

Indeed, the flame at the end of the torch began to flicker, causing the outline of their shadows to shake and quiver on the walls to either side. Before the light faded to almost nothing, however, they were able to spy a faint light up ahead.

"That's the bottom. From there you can go to many different chambers," Friar Michael whispered.

"We'd best be careful."

As they approached the end of the tunnel, they carefully peered out into a large, empty room. Torches were hung around the walls illuminating the chamber. All was still. The openings of five other tunnels could be seen from where they were hiding.

"The coast is clear," Isabella whispered.

"If I remember correctly, the way to the prisoner cells is through that tunnel over there," Friar Michael said as he pointed to the fourth tunnel entrance. "They once brought me here to get me to join and gave me a tour of the place. But after I had difficulty in going into some of the tunnels, they told me they didn't want me."

"Allah help us," Isabella whispered to herself.

The Friar and Isabella walked as quickly as they could across the roughly tiled floor and entered the third tunnel. This one was well lit with torches every few paces. Small doors lined the walls at equal intervals.

"What's behind those doors?" Isabella asked.

"You don't want to know," the Friar responded ominously.

"Oh," shrugged Isabella.

After going a little farther down the tunnel, the Friar froze in his tracks, causing Isabella to almost bump into him. From somewhere ahead muffled wailing and crying could be heard. It sounded as if many people were moaning and crying in pain and agony all at once.

"My God," whispered Isabella excitedly. "What is that pitiful screaming?"

"The priests are *convincing* people that Christianity is the right religion."

"We have to save them!"

"We can't. We would just be captured and then get tortured ourselves. All we can do is look for Umar and hope for the best."

Isabella swallowed hard and could barely ignore the screaming cries of torment. She put her hands to her ears to block the sound, but was only partially successful. Friar Michael, meanwhile, began to look at the doors on either side of the hall.

"What are you looking for?"

"I'm trying to see which doors look like they're being used. There's no point in trying the doors that have cobwebs and dust on them, like the ones we already passed. Here, help me look."

Isabella, thankful for any distraction to take her focus off the screams of the pitiful people being tortured somewhere ahead began to examine the doors in earnest. She came upon a door that might have been opened recently and lifted the locking mechanism. "Here's a door, Friar Michael," she said while opening it.

But before the Friar could respond, a gnarled, rotted old hand thrust out of the door towards Isabella, grabbing her robe and pulling her in. *"Uuuuuuun,"* a voice called from inside. *"Fooood. Heeeeelp meee. Uuuuunn."*

Isabella screamed as the ragged hand pulled her towards the darkened chamber. Friar Michael came just in time and knocked the hand off of Isabella's robe. Slamming the door shut as quickly as he could, he relocked the latch and then the moans inside drifted away.

Isabella coughed and heaved forward at the waist in revulsion. After a few minutes of shaking she managed to ask, "*Wha..*What *was that?"*

"***That,***" he answered, "was no longer human. Some poor souls have been locked in these tiny, dark cells for years. It would have killed you and fed upon your body."

"You can open the doors from now on," she stammered.

After examining a few more doors, they came upon one that had an "X" carved in it. It also looked as if it had been used fairly recently. Friar Michael put his ear up to it and listened. He could hear moans of pain, but he couldn't tell if it was the man they sought for. There were also other, strange sounds coming from inside.

"I don't know if this is the right one," the Friar said. "Let's try further on."

"Wait a minute," Isabella said. "Let me listen." When she put her ear to the moldy wooden door she too heard the grunts of pain, but at the same time, she began to recognize a different sound. It was the familiar sound she had heard in Father Peter's house when Umar began his presentation with a reading from the Qur'an. Someone was reciting Qur'anic verses inside!

"Umar," she whispered as loud as she could. "Umar, are you there?"

The sound paused and then a moment later a weak voice called out, "It is I. Who is out there? Open the door!"

Isabella unlatched the lock and swung the door open. Inside lay a badly bruised and beaten Umar. The light made his eyes squint and he used his arm to shield his face.

"It's me. It's Isabella. I brought help."

"*Isabella,*" he repeated weakly. "Thank Allah. How did you get here?"

"Let's worry about that later," she answered. "First we have to get you out of here. Come on!"

Umar crawled out of the cell revealing the extent of his injuries. He could only limp and dried blood covered his cheeks and back.

"I'm afraid I've seen better days," he said. "I apologize for my appearance."

"It's okay. I just thank God that you're safe." When he heard her say that name he managed to smile and look her in the face. She smiled back and then he noticed Friar Michael standing to the side.

"Who's this?"

"This is Friar Michael. He's here to help us."

"We had better make a quick exit," the Friar said, as he looked back down the hall. "The screams are diminishing, so they're probably done torturing for the night. They'll be bringing the prisoners back to their cells."

The three began to return the way they came and made good progress. Friar Michael let Umar lean on him. He proved to be a steady handhold for the wounded man.

At long last they emerged from the fourth tunnel into the main chamber. They were about to enter the passageway leading to the outside when a huge door slid down, blocking the way out.

"We're found out!" cried the Friar. "Run down another tunnel!"

But before they could reach any other tunnel, large wood and steel grated doors descended over each one. They were trapped.

"Heh, heh, heh," came a demented laugh from some unknown place. "Look what we have here: fresh souls to save! Guards! Take them!"

One of the doors opened up and twelve armored men emerged with large-handled swords pointed forward. They motioned for the three to move down their tunnel and then flanked them on all sides.

Umar looked at Isabella and whispered, "Be strong. The reward for one who dies in the cause of Allah is *Paradise*."

"I believe in Allah, and I want you to teach me how to live as a Muslim."

He smiled at her with soft eyes but then winced in pain as one of the guards punched him in the back. Isabella looked on horrified and then was pushed forward in a single file line. The three prisoners were marched off to a large, dark cell. All three of them were roughly shoved inside. After the door was bolted shut behind them, a small, sliding grate in the top of the door opened. Two eyes peered in at them as they stood near the back wall.

"My Isabella," a voice said. She knew that voice.

"Father!" She yelled. "What is all this? Why are you doing this to us?"

"This is the only way you can give up the demons who have turned you from your religion. Impurity is cleansed by fire. I only want what's best for you. Tomorrow you shall either renounce Islam or be burned at the stake."

Isabella recoiled in horror. Umar caught her in his arms and steadied her.

"As for you, infidel with the slick tongue," the Cardinal glared. "I shall take great pleasure in watching your limbs torn from your body on the rack. And Friar Michael - my *dear, fat* friar. You will be locked in a cell and never fed again. We shall see how long your blubber will sustain you."

"All I need is prayer for my food," said the Friar defiantly.

The Cardinal glowered at them and spit in the cell. "Tomorrow, you shall not be so courageous. Enjoy your last hours together because none of you shall ever see the light of day again!" The grate slid shut, and the cell was plunged in darkness.

The three slowly lowered themselves to the floor and all was silent. After an hour the Friar fell asleep. "Umar," Isabella asked. "How does a person become a Muslim?"

Umar began to explain the way in which a person accepts Islam. When he had finished, Isabella said, "I want to be a Muslim. Allah has answered my call for guidance."

Before she could say anything further, however, footsteps could be heard outside the cell door. Umar shook the Friar gently awake and covered his mouth, so he wouldn't say anything.

The footsteps stopped in front of their door and a moment later the grate slid open.

"What do you want now?" Umar snapped. "It's not yet tomorrow."

"*Isabella,*" a voice called. "Are you in there?"

"Yes, who's there?" she answered, quite puzzled.

The grate slid shut again and a moment later the locking bolt unhinged, and the door was pushed open. As the light from a torch flooded the cell, all three prisoners covered their eyes. Two short monks walked in and crouched before Isabella.

"Are you taking me to burn at the stake now?" she asked them with a hint of contempt in her voice.

"Don't be silly," one of the monks said. Then the pair of monks pulled back their brown hoods to reveal two girls very familiar to Isabella.

"*Maria! Rosa!*" she cried. "What are you doing here?"

"We're here *saving you*!" Rosa whispered. "Now be quiet and come on. There's not much time."

Maria helped Umar to his feet and together all five exited the cell as fast as they could. They jogged as well as they could down the tunnel until they reached the main chamber. All the steel and wood doors were up allowing them to enter the tunnel leading to the outside. The Friar grabbed a torch off the chamber wall before following the rest and after some minutes, the party emerged into the crisp, cool air of early morning.

Isabella breathed in a gulp of clean air and savored its freshness. What a change after being in that dank, dark dungeon. "Where are the guards?" She asked.

"Don't worry about them," a man said as he emerged from behind a broken wall. It was a Muslim soldier! "They won't be rising in this life ever again."

"Sheikh Samir said he wouldn't send any soldiers unless our mission failed," Isabella exclaimed.

"He didn't send any *soldiers*. He sent only *one soldier* and I'm *undercover*. Anyway, I was only to escort these women here whom the Sheikh asked me to help." With that said, the soldier turned his back and brought six horses forward.

"I guess I knew about this place from my father," Maria confessed. "He once brought me here when I was little, before the Order made it their headquarters. When the Sheikh asked to see Rosa and myself, we didn't know what he wanted, but when he said you were in trouble, I had to volunteer my help."

"I just came along to make sure Maria didn't get lost," laughed Rosa.

"We must leave now." The Muslim soldier announced hurriedly. "They will discover your absence soon, and I don't relish the thought of fighting dozens by myself."

Just as the six mounted their horses, a shout rang from inside the secret entrance, "They're gone! Assemble! Find them!"

The soldier led the Friar, Umar and the three young women at a gallop back towards Cordoba. "It's a three-hour ride!" the soldier shouted back. "We have to press on or they will surely overtake us!"

Before they emerged from the valley, the prediction proved to be a possibility. Men holding torches high could be seen following after them. Isabella looked back and thought she saw her father among them!

Horses were being brought to the men and quickly they mounted for the chase. Isabella turned her eyes forward and brushed her horse's mane firmly. If one of their horses tired or stumbled, she thought, they would lose all hope of escape!

14
The Cardinal

The Muslim soldier led the group at a grueling pace. The men of the Order were hot on their heels and had the advantage of fresh horses. By contrast, these horses had already traveled three hours *to* the old monastery, now they had to run at top speed *back* to Cordoba. After half an hour, the pursuers came within a hundred yards of the fugitives.

The Muslim soldier looked back. He saw the Friar's horse falling behind. Umar, too, looked like he was also too worn out to continue at this pace. He had been badly tortured by the Order's priests and needed rest. Looking in front of him, there was nothing but clear level grassland all the way back to the city. If only their attackers were slowed a bit, their party might make it.

The soldier slowed his mount a bit until he was riding alongside Umar. "My brother," he shouted past the wind, "I'm going to slow them down! Don't stop until you bring your group within sight of the city. Help will be waiting there!"

"No, my brother!" Umar called back, but before he could finish his words, the valiant Muslim soldier halted his white horse and turned abruptly to face the enraged warrior-priests. He stood his ground silently and with determination as the thirty or more men bore down on his position. When they were almost upon him, he raised his sword high in the air and yelled the battle cry of Muslims everywhere, "***Allahu Akbar!***" Then he charged his horse straight at the rushing war party.

His first pass caused the Order's men to scatter, and he managed to fell one opponent with a clean strike along his chest. The rest of the horsemen doubled back and surrounded him. Slowly the circle tightened.

Umar looked back only in time to see a riderless horse running away into the grassy fields. *"Allah grant him the highest place in Paradise,"* he whispered, as a tear tore itself from his eye. But the man had not died in vain. The lead was so great now that the Order could never overtake them before they reached the walls of Cordoba. All that was needed now was speed.

When he saw his prey getting away, one of the priests flung his black cloak to the ground and snarled angrily. It was the Cardinal. Rage and anger filled his heart as he saw his daughter escaping with Umar. "The flesh!" he cried. *"Destroy the flesh!"*

He raised his bloody sword high, freshly stained with the blood of the Muslim soldier. "After them!" he commanded. His men obeyed instantly and resumed the chase.

As they passed over fields and through farmland, the morning sun continued to rise higher into the sky. Their horses were sweating profusely and straining under the urgency of their riders. Suddenly, Friar Michael's mount stumbled in sheer exhaustion and threw its rider to the ground. The Friar landed with a thump and quickly struggled to his feet.

The others stopped their mounts and galloped to where he fell. Isabella, Maria and Rosa all dismounted to help him up. Umar tried to get off his horse but tumbled to the ground in pain. His wounds were still affecting him and causing great difficulty. He closed his eyes and asked Allah for strength.

The three girls managed to pull the Friar to his feet again and held him firmly. Umar was somehow able to regain stand as well. The Friar's horse, which was limping off into the distance, seemed horribly out of reach. It was then that they saw that their own steeds were too tired to resume the flight. Now close enough to make out individual faces, the frightened and weary fugitives could see the mounted priests heading straight for them, scowling. They had to move fast.

"Come on!" cried Isabella. "We'll make it! Let's run! Don't give up!"

The five people set out again on foot as fast as they could. Maria helped the Friar while Rosa and Isabella gave Umar a hand. They made it up and over the top of a grassy hill and saw a small depression in the land ahead of them. As they plunged down the hill they could hear the galloping of many horses approaching closer and closer.

They had scarcely reached the bottom of the hill and not even begun their climb up the grassy knoll to the other side when from behind them came an eerie sound. The cackle of cruel laughter echoed through the air and the tired group looked back to see a line of horsemen on the ridge above, nearly thirty in all, standing in a long line, side by side.

"We have you now, infidels!" cried the Cardinal, with his fist raised. "Get them!" he screamed.

At his command, the enraged horsemen moved together at once in a charge down the hill towards their helpless victims below. Isabella looked at the climb above her and knew they would never make it. She hated her meaningless death and swore that she would die fighting. Umar and the Friar stood themselves in front of the girls so they would be the first to face the riders and Rosa and Maria stood off to the side.

Isabella surprised both men, however, when she took up a position between both of them. She looked at the Friar, and then at Umar. She was determined. She knew she would die. At the top of her lungs she cried the words she had heard uttered so many times before by others. But now they were her words, her faith. As loud as she could she cried out, *"Allahu Akbar!"* Then she faced the oncoming horsemen with gritted teeth.

But to her surprise, her cry seemed to echo louder and louder through the valley. It took a moment for her to realize that it was not her voice that was echoing, but the voices of hundreds of men somewhere behind her. She looked back and saw a wondrous sight. On the hill above stood a line of Muslim soldiers, all gleaming in their polished armor and shields.

"Allahu Akbar!" they shouted, as their commander ordered his men to charge. Down they came into the valley like water rushing over a waterfall. Muslims coming to fight the foes and save the oppressed!

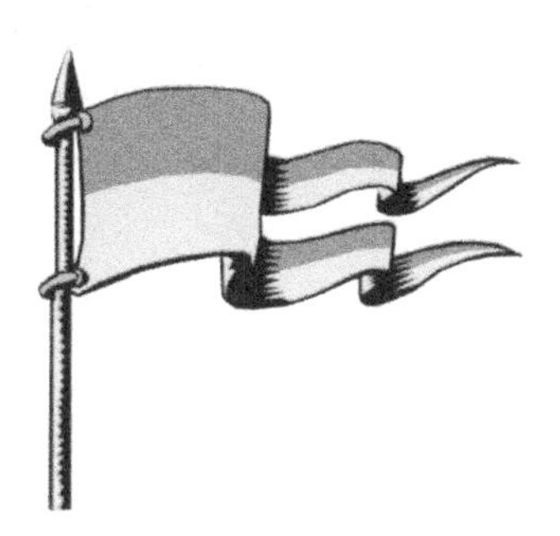

When the Cardinal saw victory being snatched from his grasp, he flew into a blind rage and charged with madness into the battle. A regiment of the Muslim soldiers surrounded Umar's group and protected them from the maddening assault. The rest of the Muslim unit engaged the priests in battle, and a general melee of hand-to-hand combat ensued.

Swords flew and shields were splintered! Men fought and died, and horses ran away without their riders. A few of the warrior-priests attempted a unified charge at Isabella and her group, but they were pushed back by the fearless Muslims protecting them.

After a few more minutes of confusion, sword-play and open battle, the remaining warrior-priests, now badly outnumbered, turned and fled. Though some were captured and quickly bound with rope.

When the Muslim commander, a young dark-skinned man with deep coal eyes, approached the ragged group of fugitives, he addressed Umar first, *"Assalamu alaikum, Brother."*

Umar, joined by Isabella replied, *"Wa alaikum assalam."*

The soldiers then helped them all to their feet and took them, along with the captured priests, to the city which lay just over the hill. Victory was achieved but the trouble was not quite finished yet.

15

Peaceful Surrender

Umar spent the next few days in the hospital along with Friar Michael, but they made a speedy recovery. Isabella, Maria and Rosa, in the meantime, were guests of Sheikh Samir's wife, Hajjah [27] Munira. When they were ready to leave the hospital, Umar, the Friar and the three young women were summoned to the official court of Cordoba.

When they entered the main courtroom, they found it filled with spectators. The Qadi, or judge, was seated behind a table in the front of the court room. An attendant led the five to sit on chairs in the front. None of them knew why they were there. A moment later, the Qadi recited, *"Bismillah al Rahman al Rahim,"* [28] and the court was brought to session.

Sheikh Samir entered the courtroom and sat near Umar and the others. He smiled at Isabella and shook hands with Friar Michael. A moment later, a guard entered from another door. Behind him walked the Cardinal. His hands were in cuffs, and he shuffled

---

[27] Hajjah is an honorific title for a woman who has completed the pilgrimage to Mecca.
[28] "In the Name of Allah, the Compassionate Source of All Mercy."

arrogantly. He was made to sit in a chair on the opposite side of Umar and the others. The guard stood at attention near the wall.

The Cardinal looked at Umar and then Isabella and grimaced angrily. The Qadi began to speak, "Brothers and sisters and all who are living under the protection of the Islamic state. We are here to settle the case which was brought before me by the request of the Cardinal of Cordoba. Being that the Christians of this city are Dhimmis and have agreed to pay taxes in exchange for protection and equal status before the law, we must grant this hearing as is due upon us."

The Cardinal smirked.

"Cardinal, you are accused of causing harm to Muslims and Christians. You may state your case first."

The man slowly rose to his feet and addressed the Qadi, "*Gracious Judge*. I stand here, a man in chains and under arrest, while I am, in fact, the one who was wronged. My daughter was seduced unlawfully by the man you see sitting here in this room." He pointed towards Umar.

"What you're saying is a grave accusation." The Qadi responded.

"But it's true. All I have done is what any father would do to protect his daughter from the onslaught of an unprincipled and ruthless man."

"Very well," the Qadi exclaimed. "Umar AbdulHakim. You have been accused of trying to seduce a Christian girl without right or permission. You may state your case."

Umar stood up and responded, "I have only been guilty of engaging in a dialogue with seekers after knowledge. As you are well aware, I was invited to two gatherings of Christians and brought to light the truth of Islam and the falsity of Christian beliefs. For this I was attacked, kidnapped, tortured and abused. I stand before Allah an innocent man."

"Sheikh Samir," the Qadi announced, "you have been granted permission by the Amir to present certain evidence which is relevant to this case. You may proceed."

The old Sheikh stood up and walked to the clear space in front of the Qadi's table. He turned to face the court and said, "Allah says in the Holy Qur'an, '*Truth hurls against lies and knocks out its brains*.' And indeed the truth will manifest itself here today, Insha'llah.

"A young Christian girl named Isabella sought to engage Muslims in a dialogue with Christians. During the course of this dialogue, she found that the beliefs of her father were not reasonable and were obviously man-made. For this discovery, she was abused and threatened. Our Brother, Umar, who was instrumental in her Islamic education, was then kidnapped by a secret Christian terrorist organization called the Order of the Inquisition, and he was duly tortured and held a prisoner until Isabella, her two friends Maria and Rosa and a fine Christian Friar named Michael came to his rescue.

"During the course of this rescue attempt, a volunteer Muslim soldier, a man by the name of Abdullah, was made a martyr at the hands of the Cardinal." Sheikh Samir raised an accusing finger at the Cardinal and all eyes in the court turned on him.

"Furthermore, this man and his organization operate a secret torture facility where they harm people who are interested in becoming Muslim. We have only recently learned of its location and sent an army unit there. They freed many prisoners and found horrors unimaginable by any sane human being.

"To end this evidence, I submit that the Cardinal led a group of armed men on a chase against these innocent persons and many Muslim soldiers were wounded in beating off their furious assault. I rest my case."

"Do you have anything to say in your defense, *Cardinal*?" the Qadi asked.

"I am the Cardinal of Cordoba. Leader of all the Christians of this city. My daughter and her friends are Christians, and by your own law they must be returned to me to be dealt with as I see fit. I demand Isabella, Maria and Rosa be turned over to me, and that I should be released immediately."

"Yes, it is true. A Christian must be turned over to Christian authorities when religious matters are concerned," the Qadi agreed.

Isabella stood up and announced, "Respectful Qadi, may I say something?"

The Qadi gravely nodded his head, "Yes."

"It is true, I am a Christian right now. But I do not believe in the Christian religion. I have, upon much thought, found that its teachings are against logic and cannot be supported, even by the Bible itself. Jesus was a Messenger of God, but I cannot believe he was also a god too. Furthermore, I realize the Bible is not the inspired word of God, but a collection of many people's opinions and stories. Therefore, I would like to publicly declare, that *there is no god but Allah and that Muhammad is the Messenger of Allah."*

The courtroom erupted in cries of *"Allahu Akbar!" "Allahu Akbar!"*

It took several minutes for the Qadi to restore order. Isabella, still standing, turned to her friends, Maria and Rosa. They looked up at her and smiled. Then they both stood up and each took one of Isabella's hands in theirs. In loud and clear voices, they also declared, *"There is no god but Allah, and Muhammad is the Messenger of Allah."*

Again, the cries of joy flooded forth from the assembled people. The Cardinal scowled and gnashed his teeth in anger.

"There you have it," the Qadi said to the Cardinal. "They have declared their acceptance of Islam and are now entitled to the full protection of the Islamic nation. You have no case any longer. You will stand trial for the murder of the Muslim soldier, Abdullah, as well as for running an illegal terrorist organization. All of your property will be confiscated and turned over to your daughter and you will be removed from your position as Cardinal. The Christian community will have to choose a new one. Until then, I propose that Friar Michael fill that office. Case closed!"

The Qadi slammed his wooden mallet on the table signaling that the court was adjourned. The Muslims rushed forward to celebrate this wonderful victory and several Muslim sisters offered silken scarves for their three new Muslim sisters to wear.

Isabella and her two friends were whisked away by the joyful women, and Umar, Sheikh Samir and Friar Michael were carried on the shoulders of the men out of the courthouse. The Cardinal, however, was left frowning, as he was led back to his prison cell.

Sometime later, Umar proposed marriage to Isabella, and she accepted immediately. They were wed in an open-air ceremony in the *Janaina* Garden. Sheikh Samir did the *Nikkah.* [29] Maria and Rosa, too, both found good Muslim husbands and lived a life more satisfying and spiritually aware than ever before.

Isabella went on to learn more about Islam and in time mastered Qur'anic Arabic. She completed her dream of reading the Qur'an and increased in faith everyday. Eventually, she became so skilled that she took a job in the University of Cordoba. She became a teacher of Arabic: a teacher of women - *and of men*.

May Allah let us learn from her example and build true faith within ourselves, standing up for what we believe in and opposing evil and falsehood. Ameen.

[29] Nikkah means marriage ceremony.

The End

Some Other Books by Yahiya Emerick

See more at www.amirahpublishing.com

Ahmad Deen and the Curse of the Aztec Warrior

By Yahiya Emerick

Where is he? Ahmad Deen and his sister Layla thought they were getting a nice vacation in tropical Mexico. But what they're really going to get is a hair-raising race against time to save their father from becoming the next victim of an ancient, bloody ritual! How can Ahmad save his father and deal with his bratty sister at the same time? To make matters worse, no one seems to want to help them find the mysterious lost city that may hold the key to their father's whereabouts. And then there's that jungle guide with the strangely familiar jacket. Are they brave enough—or crazy enough, to take on the Curse of the Aztec Warrior? Illustrated. Ages 9-14

Ahmad Deen and the Jinn at Shaolin

By Yahiya Emerick

A once in a lifetime chance! Ahmad Deen is one of ten lucky students in his school who gets an all-expense paid trip to China. But instead of *getting* a history lesson, Ahmad may become a victim *of* history as he is thrust in the middle of a bizarre web of superstition, corruption and ancient hatreds that seek to destroy all who interfere. Who kidnapped his room-mate? What clue can only be found in the Shaolin Temple? How will Ahmad learn the Kung-Fu skills he'll need to defeat the powers of darkness. or will he fall prey to the mysterious *Jinn at Shaolin?* Illustrated. Ages 9-14

Layla Deen and the Case of the Ramadan Rogue

By Yahiya Emerick

Somebody's trying to ruin her Ramadan! Layla Deen and her family were just settling in to break a long day's fast when their mother came running from the kitchen and cried, "*Someone stole the food for Iftar!*" Layla knew it was a terrible crime and decided to get to the bottom of this mystery. See what happens! Illustrated. Ages 7-12

Layla Deen and the Popularity Contest

By Yahiya Emerick

Who could have done that? Layla Deen is just trying to survive her last year in junior high. But when someone enters her into the school-wide popularity contest, her world is thrown into confusion. Did her best friend betray her? How can she measure up to all those popular girls? Why was she assigned as a peer tutor to a girl who lived a life of self-destruction? Check this story out and see how Layla deals with all this and more. Illustrated. 130 pages. Ages 10-16

The Seafaring Beggar and Other Tales

By Yahiya Emerick

A delightful collection of short stories, poems, essays and other writings that showcase a variety of themes and inspirational nuggets of wisdom. Many of these stories and poems have been published in international magazines and are sure to put a smile on your face and a warmth in your heart for the beauty that is Islam. Illustrated. Ages 10-14

Muslim Youth Speak: Voices of Today's Muslim Youth

By Yahiya Emerick

What do Muslim youth today think about Islam? What are their suggestions for living and promoting it? What are their observations about the state of Islam in America today and how to make it grow? This book is a compilation of essays, plays, exhortations and other writings by actual Muslim youth. Find out what's going on in the minds of the second generation! For Junior High level.

The Story of Yusuf

By Yahiya Emerick

Finally! The most beautiful story translated for today's English-speakers. Enjoy the sweep of Allah's revelation as you follow the adventures of Prophet Yusuf as he embarks on a harrowing journey that begins with betrayal and ends in a display of ultimate forgiveness. Illustrated. Ages 9-12

Full Circle: Story and Coloring Book

By Yahiya Emerick

What do you do when... Rashid is going to the Masjid for prayer. But on the way he finds an old woman who needs help. If he helps her, he will be late for prayer. If he does not help her, he will miss doing a good deed. Should he help the old woman or should he get to prayer on time? Find out what he does in this wonderful story about going full circle. A strong moral tale showing young children how to continue to do good deeds even when they are worried about keeping other responsibilities. Illustrated. Ages 5-7

In the Path of the Holy Prophet

By Yahiya Emerick

A collection of 57 sayings of the Prophet Muhammad on subjects related to spirituality, meditation, the other world and how to live rightly. Fully illustrated to enhance the impact of the text. For Junior High and High School level.

The Holy Qur'an for School Children: Juz 'Amma

By Yahiya Emerick

A complete textbook for learning and understanding the last section of the Holy Qur'an. Every surah is presented with an engaging introduction, a clear explanatory translation for maximum comprehension, review questions and activities to test the knowledge of the students on the themes of each surah, the full Arabic text and finally, a phonics-based transliteration system is given which is the easiest method for pronouncing the sounds of the Arabic text. Illustrated. Ages 8-16

Color and Learn Salah

By Yahiya Emerick

A complete guide to learning how to do prayers combined in a coloring book format. Covers the complete prayer including ablutions, supplications and movements. Illustrated. Ages 6-8

How to Tell Others About Islam

By Yahiya Emerick

A manual of technique, advice and inspiration on how to communicate Islam to non- Muslims. Topics include how to approach different ethnic groups in North America, how to prepare for giving da'wah, how to handle other religions, as well as many others. Several appendices offer lists of the most effective and readable Islamic literature currently available in English. Illustrated. For High School level.

My First Book About Eman
By Yahiya Emerick

A first-grade textbook on Islam that lays a solid groundwork for children in learning their faith and the reasons why it is important. Lessons are friendly, focused and provide excellent starting points for further enrichment and exploration of the faith. Illustrated. Ages 5-6

My First Book About Islam
By Yahiya Emerick

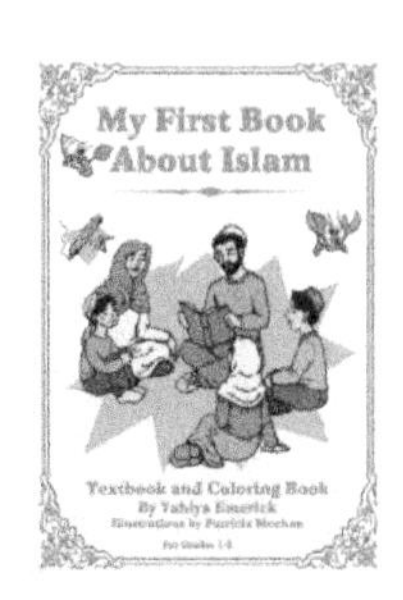

This is the second grade textbook on Islam that builds upon the lessons taught in the first grade textbook. The Islamic worldview is introduced with an emphasis on learning the basics of Islamic religious duties and practices as well as what it means to be a Muslim. Illustrated. Ages 6-7

Learning About Islam
By Yahiya Emerick

This textbook covers all the fundamentals of Islam and is arranged into clearly defined lessons and units. Review exercises at the end of each lesson provide ready-made homework assignments and unit review exercises prepare students for unit tests. A stunningly beautiful book by the same author as the popular textbook for older children, "What Islam is All About." Illustrated. Ages 10-12

What Islam is All About
By Yahiya Emerick

The standard textbook on Islam for grades 7 to Adult in much of the English-speaking world. This book covers all the major beliefs, practices and related material that would make one well-versed in the Islamic way of life. These fascinating lessons introduce students to a variety of aspects of Islamic belief and history that makes Islam relevant and fun. Illustrated. Ages 13-Adult

A Journey through the Holy Qur'an
By Yahiya Emerick

A modern free-flowing translation that addresses the needs of the modern-day youth. Easy to read and with helpful background information on the various passages of the holy book. 12-adult.

The Complete Idiot's Guide to Rumi Meditations
By Yahiya Emerick

An exploration into the Islamic dimensions of Rumi's life and thought. This book presents many of Rumi's poems that relate to the Islamic way of life and discusses how to draw faith-lessons from his voluminous work. An excellent book for Junior high school to adult.

Muhammad
By Yahiya Emerick

The story of the Prophet Muhammad told in the form of a narrative. This biography has been acclaimed as the most balanced and easiest to read book of its type on many websites all over the internet! Step back in time as you enter 7th century Arabia and find out why. For High School level to adult.

The Holy Qur'an as If you Were There
By Yahiya Emerick

The Holy Qur'an for teenagers and young adults. A version for younger children is also available called, "The Meaning of the Holy Qur'an for School Children."

The Complete Idiot's Guide to Understanding Islam

By Yahiya Emerick

A complete overview of Islam and its worldview in an easy-to-access format and style. Excellent for high school through adult reading levels and also great for *da'wah*. Illustrated.

The Meaning of the Holy Qur'an in Today's English

By Yahiya Emerick

Finally, a modern translation and commentary that fills the needs of the present while paying due respect to the understandings and methodologies of our pious predecessors. This work contains reasons for revelation, voluminous footnotes and commentary as well as a large number of extremely useful resources – all encompassed by a flowing and natural style of modern English. Ages 16-adult.

Made in the USA
Monee, IL
24 October 2021

80702488R00083